Megan the KLUTZ

Megan the KLUTZ

Alida Young

Published by Willowisp Press, Inc.
401 E. Wilson Bridge Road, Worthington, Ohio 43085

Printed in the United States of America

10 9 8 7 6

ISBN 0-87406-146-6

*To my brother, John Quick,
for all his encouragement and help.*

*And to my friend Peggy
for having faith in me.*

*A very special thanks to
the fifth and sixth graders
at Ramona Elementary School
in Hawthorne, California.*

One

DO you ever have days when you feel as if you have three feet and seven extra fingers...on each hand? And the neighbor kid calls you a klutz? And your mom bawls you out again for daydreaming when you're supposed to be working? And your sister gives you a hard time just because you left some gum in the pocket of her favorite pair of jeans and they went through the wash?

Well, if you do, then you know how I feel practically every day. Sometimes I think I can't do anything right. I mean, I can make delicate jewelry to sell in our gift shop. I can string these tiny little silver and turquoise beads without dropping a single one. Then I manage to catch my finger in the cash register or in the credit card machine. How do you figure it?

Why can't I be like my sister, Trish?

Mom, Trish, my eighteen-year-old sister, and I run a gallery and gift shop. A lot of the paintings in the gallery were done by my dad. He doesn't live with us anymore—well, I don't want to think about that.

Today, I was stuck here in the workroom making a necklace for Mrs. Simpson. I had to watch the shop while my mom was at the bank and Trish was taking dance lessons. I'd much rather have been painting my weird little characters on rocks that I collect down by the river. It isn't really art, though. They're not like my dad's paintings or my mother's sculpture or Trish's dancing. I've never even shown my dumb rocks to anybody. I wish there were just one thing I could do better than Trish. Anything.

My back was getting tired from working on the necklace, so I leaned back and closed my eyes.

The limousine pulls up in front of the White House. The beautiful, talented Megan Steele is to receive an award from the President of the United States. . . .

The jingle of the bell on the front door of the gallery jolted me out of my daydream. I hurried out front and bumped into the corner of a glass cabinet that held jewelry. Then somehow I managed to catch the pocket of my work smock on a display rack.

"May I help you?" I asked, rubbing my sore hip bone. Then I recognized Mrs. Rhodes. The Rhodes family founded San Angelo, but none of them have lived here for years. They come to visit every summer. And every summer I dream that Christopher Rhodes will notice me.

Megan, where have you been hiding all these years? I can't believe I'd miss a pretty face like yours. . . .

"Megan, how you've grown, child. How old are you now?" Mrs. Rhodes asked as she looked around at the paintings. "Twelve?"

I gritted my teeth. I'd told Mom the dumb pink smock made me look like a baby. "I'm fourteen, Mrs. Rhodes."

Oh, my beloved, where shall we go tonight? The moon is full. The air is warm and filled with the fragrance of orange blossoms. Let us dance under the stars. . . .

"We've bought the Enright mansion," Mrs. Rhodes said. "We're planning to live here permanently."

I managed to keep from squealing. I was dying to ask her if Chris was back in town, too. One year he'd spent the summer in England. Another year he went to summer camp in Maine. I didn't ask her, though. I didn't want to appear too interested.

Mrs. Rhodes was looking at my dad's paintings, going from one to another, talking half to herself. "This one could go in the library. It's about the right size. And this one is a perfect color for the dining room."

I could feel the anger churning in my stomach. She was more interested in the sizes and colors than how great my dad's paintings were. It really burned me.

"Christopher and I will be back in tomorrow to select a couple," Mrs. Rhodes said.

So, he was in town. Maybe this would be my year.

I watched Mrs. Rhodes leave the shop and climb into a limousine like the one in my fantasy. I mean, I've seen school buses that were smaller. I could hardly wait for Mom to come back so I could tell Carla and Helen Mae the great news. All three of us have had a crush on Chris since we were eleven. I closed my eyes and sighed dreamily.

The beautiful Megan Steele steps gracefully into the long, black limousine. She settles back against the soft cushions and turns to her companion. "Where are we going?" she asks.

"I just purchased the Enright mansion," the prince says in his deep, thrilling voice. "I hope it meets with your approval."

"Megan, why are you standing there in the

middle of the gallery?"

I whirled around. Mom had come in the back way. "Oh, no reason," I said quickly. "I was just thinking about the Rhodes family. They're going to live here. Mom, can I take my break now? I want to meet Carla and Helen Mae and tell them."

"Did you finish the necklace for Mrs. Simpson?"

"Almost. I stopped for a minute. Working on it gave me such a headache." I held my hand to my temple and gave a long, exaggerated sigh.

Oh, doctor, not a brain tumor! Will you have to shave off all my hair? How long will I live, doctor? Tell me, I can take it. A year? Six months? A half hour?

"Megan Lynn Steele!"

"What?" I asked, startled out of my daydream.

Mom gave a sigh that was even longer and deeper than mine had been. "I said, don't be gone longer than a half hour."

"I won't. Thanks, Mom."

"Be careful of the traffic," she said — as usual.

Do mothers ever stop saying, "Be careful!" "Don't drop that." "Wear a sweater"?

I tugged off the smock, grabbed my bag, and headed for the door.

"Watch that stand!"

Picture postcards flew everywhere.

"Mom, isn't there a better place for these cards than right by the door?"

She gave me "the look." I get this look from a lot of people.

I picked up the cards and put them back on the rack. Then I hurried across to Yokomura's Pizza Palace. The main highway runs right through town, so all the businesses are on each side of the road. In Yokomura's window was a large poster. It had a picture of Trish and the words, VOTE FOR TRISH STEELE FOR MISS SAN ANGELO. Mr. Yokomura is Trish's sponsor.

I stared at her picture. Sometimes I wish she'd get a pimple or grow a wart. Trish has golden hair and sea-green eyes. My hair is ordinary old brown, and my eyes are hazel. Now what kind of color is hazel? Trish gets great tans; I sunburn. Trish plans to be a ballerina; I trip over my own feet. Trish is beautiful, glamorous, and cool. I'm a klutz. Life just isn't fair.

I made a face at her picture and muttered "Blaaagh" under my breath.

The wind was cold for June. But inside the Pizza Palace, the warm, pungent air felt good. All the kids hang out in Yokomura's.

"Hi, Megan," Andy Gerritson said from behind the counter.

I like Andy. He's like an old sweater—you know, kind of warm and comfortable. He has sandy hair and gray eyes. And sometimes you forget he's in the room.

"Hiiii, Meg."

That was jerky Spud Walters, who lives next door to me. His parents own the San Angelo Motel. He was spinning around on the stool. He's a real pain. I don't know how Andy can stand to have him hanging around all the time. Spud got his nickname because he was always eating raw potatoes. Mom insists that he's obnoxious because he's unsure of himself. Ha!

"My name is Megan, not Meg," I told him for the millionth time. I don't know why I bother to correct him.

I headed for the back where Carla Townsend was waiting for me. As I slid my long legs under the table, I cracked my ankle on the chair leg—as usual.

"You're late," Carla said.

"I'm not a lady of leisure like you." I'd read that somewhere and had been waiting to use it on Carla. She never has any work to do except to keep her room in order. I envy her.

I brushed back a flyaway hair that had come loose from my ponytail.

13

"You should get rid of that ponytail," Carla said. "Nobody wears them."

"It keeps my hair out of my face when I'm working," I said a little sharply. She's been harping about my ponytail for ages.

"Why don't you get a cut like mine?" Carla asked, smoothing her shiny black hair.

"Mine doesn't have any body." I hate this baby-fine hair.

Just then Helen Mae Vorchek came running in. Carla muttered, "Why does she insist on wearing those terrible T-shirts? She looks positively disgusting, bouncing up and down that way."

I just wished I had more to bounce up and down.

Oh, sure, maybe Helen Mae is a little overweight and doesn't try to do much with her looks, but I like her.

"Sorry I'm late," Helen Mae gasped, and plumped onto the seat. "At the last minute I had to change the baby."

Carla usually has something sarcastic to say about Helen Mae's mother having had another baby at thirty-nine. I broke in before she thought of something. "Guess what? Have I ever got a piece of news."

"Me first," Carla said. "My news is important. Christopher Rhodes is moving to

14

San Angelo, and he's going to live here year-round."

"Oh, I may die," Helen Mae said. "I've been in love with him forever."

"Now, what's your news?" Carla asked me.

"Nothing," I said glumly. Just once I'd like to beat Carla at something.

Andy came over to our table. "What'll you have?" he asked. And with a flourish, he set three glasses of water on the table.

Carla wanted a diet soda. Helen Mae ordered her usual hot fudge sundae. I decided on pizza. "Make it extra cheesy."

"How about one of Mr. Yokomura's latest creations?" Andy asked. "It's topped with raw fish and seaweed."

"You're kidding."

"He's even toying with the idea of a squid and octopus pizza."

I gulped. "Plain cheese, thanks."

As soon as Andy left, Helen Mae said, "I have news, too." She paused for effect. "I'm thinking of trying out for Mrs. Gerritson's play this year."

Carla snickered. "You! What do you know about acting?"

Sometimes I wonder why the three of us hang around together. We've been neighbors and friends so long it's a habit, I guess.

"I think it's a great idea, Helen Mae," I told her.

Carla quickly changed the subject. "Did you know the Rhodes are buying the Enright mansion?"

"No," Helen Mae said. "I was in it once, and it's fabulous. I'll bet it has twenty bedrooms, all with their own baths."

Christopher, my beloved husband, I really need a new bathroom. All twenty are just too, too small. It would be lovely to have a tub as large as an Olympic-sized pool. . . .

"He's coming in right now," Andy said as he placed a wedge of pizza in front of me.

"Who's coming in?" I asked.

"The guy you three have been drooling over ever since you got here. Chris Rhodes."

Helen Mae squealed. Carla took a mirror out of her purse and put on fresh lip gloss. Determined to be cool and unflustered, I casually picked up the extra-cheesy pizza and took a bite. The cheese kept stringing out, and I took a larger bite to keep it from going down my chin.

"Hey, Chris, come over and meet three of your fans."

Chris is six feet tall with blond hair—a real hunk. He was dressed all in white.

Andy introduced us.

Helen Mae ducked her head and choked out a feeble, "Pleased to meet you—at last."

Carla arched her neck and gave Chris a sideways look. "We met in the parade last year. I'm Mayor Townsend's daughter."

Chris nodded and turned to me.

I had tried to swallow the pizza before Chris had reached our table. Long strings of cheese drizzled from my chin. As I tried to pull them loose, they stuck to my fingers, to my hair, to the napkin. I was choking. I couldn't breathe. I tried to say *Help me!* But I couldn't make a sound. Panicked now, tears welled up in my eyes.

Before I knew what was happening, Andy quickly pulled me up. He bent me over, grabbed me under the rib cage, and gave a push inward and up. A piece of pizza shot out of my mouth and landed right on Chris's white shorts.

"Oh, yuck," Carla said. "That's really gross."

I gasped for breath and held my chest. I was afraid some ribs were broken.

"Are you okay?" Andy asked.

I nodded. "I think so." Then I realized what I'd done to Chris. His face was a mixture of anger and disgust. "I'm sorry." I blurted out. "I'm so sorry!"

I fumbled for my money, dropped it on the table, and without a word to anyone, I ran out.

As I leaned up against Trish's poster, I wished the ground would open up and swallow me. Then I got a mental picture of the earth choking on me and of Andy trying to stretch his arms around the world to give it the Heimlich maneuver. I saw myself rocket into the air like a shooting star and land on Chris's shorts — his white, white shorts.

I'll never, never be able to face Christopher Rhodes again. . . not ever.

Two

*L*ET *me go! Spider, let me free! The web of
mozzarella cheese clings to me, holds me
fast. The blond spider moves closer and closer,
ready to devour me. . . .*

"Megan, eat your dinner."

"I'm not hungry, Mom."

I didn't think I could eat another bite in my
entire life. I didn't want to ever look at food
again.

"I don't know how I'm going to get
everything organized in time," Mom was
saying. "I've asked six people to handle the
float entries for the parade."

I had been only half listening to Mom and
Trish talking about Festival Week. It's still
two months away. But Mom is chairman this
year, so she has lots of plans to make. It's bad
enough to have a sister like Trish. But I also
have to put up with a mother who is good at

everything. She runs the gallery and is a super cook and sculptress. We sell some of her work in the gallery. I'm scared to death I'm going to knock over one of the pedestals and break a sculpture.

"I wish we had a talent contest like the Miss America contest," Trish was saying. "How can I make the judges notice me in a group song and dance number?"

"You'll be the best dancer," Mom said.

After five years of dance classes, she ought to be good, I thought. When I was eight or nine, Carla, Helen Mae, and I took some dancing lessons. We had this really neat teacher, Erma Agler, who taught everything from tap to ballet. I thought she was beautiful. She had long red hair that she could actually sit on. And I loved the way she whirled and spun on her toes in *pointe* shoes. More than anything else in the world, I'd wanted to own a pair of pink satin *pointe* shoes and to be able to dance like Miss Agler. But she said my big toes were too long. Can you believe it? My life's dream was ruined because my big toes were too long!

At the first recital Carla got to wear a beautiful, fluffy tutu and float lightly around the stage. Not Helen Mae and me. We had to wear Dutch costumes. At the last minute Miss

Agler got sick, and her assistant got the brilliant idea that Helen Mae and I would wear wooden shoes. Boy, I hate to even think about that night. It was a disaster. We didn't get to practice in our wooden shoes, and we got our feet tangled up. We landed in a heap. We must have looked like a couple of Dutch pretzels.

Dancing definitely isn't one of my talents. In fact, I don't think I have any talents in my genes.

No, I don't want that pair of jeans. I don't care if they do have a designer's name on the pocket. I want a pair of jeans that has TALENT in every pocket. I don't care what talent. I just want to be good at something.

The sharp ring of the telephone brought me back to reality.

"That's probably Larry," Trish said, jumping up to answer the phone.

Trish is really popular. She's gone steady with a lot of different guys. This month it's Larry.

"Megan, it's for you," she said disgustedly. "Carla."

She was probably calling to needle me about what happened with Chris. I thought. "Tell her I'm in the shower. Tell her I've gone out on a date. Tell her I'm dead."

"Carla, Megan will call you later. Okay?"

"Thanks a bunch," I muttered.

Trish hung up. "What's the matter with Carla, anyway?" Trish asked. "Every time she said your name she got the giggles."

No way was I going to talk to Carla tonight.

"Megan, if you're not going to eat, you can start clearing the table," Mom said.

I was feeling too down in the dumps to even argue that it was Trish's turn to clean up. Still thinking about the fiasco with Chris, I loaded the dishes into the dishwasher and cleaned up the kitchen.

We live in a huge apartment behind the shop. Mom designed it herself, and it looks like a picture in one of those decorating magazines.

My room is always a mess. It usually looks like a garage sale in progress. Mom let me fix it up myself so it could reflect the "real me." So how does a bedroom reflect a klutz? I haven't figured that out yet.

When I finished in the kitchen, I asked if I could go over to Helen Mae's.

"Fine, dear," Mom said absently, without even looking up from a long list she was working on. "Be back before dark. And wear a jacket."

I grabbed my sweater and canvas bag and headed for Helen Mae's. Halfway to her house

I changed my mind. Carla might be there, and I just couldn't handle any of her smart remarks yet. I took off for the river.

The San Angelo River curves right around the town. We have a huge park with swimming, boating, and all sorts of things to do. My favorite spot is downstream where the river goes on a rampage. I like to sit on a rock near a waterfall and sing crazy songs at the top of my lungs. But this evening, I didn't even hum.

A fine mist was blowing off the crashing, tumbling water. The air was cool and smelled like damp earth and pine trees and—pizza! Even after taking a long shower and washing my hair three times, I still felt as if strings of cheese were clinging to me.

But after a while the sound of the waterfall made me feel better. I got out a notebook and ballpoint pen. Lately, I've been trying my hand at poetry. Maybe my talent is literary.

And for the Nobel prize in literature—Megan Steele for her poem "Lost Souls. . . ."

I balanced the notebook on my knee and began to write.

> *The waves broke high with a hiss of foam*
> *On some forgotten shore.*
> *Where souls of men are wont to roam*
> *For they will live no more.*

23

"Garbage!" I said aloud. I tore off the page and wadded it into a ball. So much for my literary talent.

I couldn't even write a dumb poem. You'd think having an artist for a father, a sculptress who can do everything for a mother, and a dancer who will probably be this year's Miss San Angelo for a sister, that I'd have one crummy talent. Maybe if I were talented or had brains or were beautiful like Trish and Mom, Dad wouldn't have divorced us, I thought, feeling more miserable than ever.

"Hey, Megan, mind if I join you?"

I nearly fell off the rock trying to see who had sneaked up on me. It was Andy. The roar of the water had covered the sound of his footsteps.

"You scared the daylights out of me," I said.

"Sorry. I saw you head for the river, so I followed. Are you okay?"

"Sure. Thanks to you. That was scary not being able to breathe. I'm sorry I ran out without thanking you."

"People never expect things like that to happen to them."

"I think I would have choked to death." I cringed, remembering. "I've never been so embarrassed. Is—uh—is Chris really mad at me?"

"Well, he wasn't exactly overjoyed. But he

doesn't have any reason to be mad at you."

"I'll never be able to look him in the face again."

"That's dumb. You couldn't help it."

"I didn't have to shove half a pizza in my mouth. When I get nervous I do stupid things. I'm a klutz."

"You know, Megan, you have a rotten attitude. If you keep thinking you're a klutzy little kid, you'll keep on acting like one."

"Since when did you become a psychiatrist?"

"I get all these neat bits of wisdom from listening to my mom. She's always saying that self-conscious people should take up acting. Why don't you try out for the play for Festival Week?"

"Me? I can't act."

"Anybody can act. You're always daydreaming and pretending, aren't you?"

"How'd you know that?"

"Because half the time you're in another world."

"I didn't think anyone had noticed."

"Mom says daydreaming is just like acting," Andy said. "You pretend to be the character you're playing, and pretty soon you forget all about yourself. Haven't you ever been in a play before?"

I groaned. He was always quoting his

mother. "Sure," I said. "Don't you remember in the first grade I played Letty Lettuce? I got so carried away with being a head of lettuce, I thought there was a big green worm on me. I messed up the whole play."

"Oh. . .yeah." He shook his head at the memory. "Miss Farnsworth was pretty upset."

"And you want *me* to try out for your mom's play?"

"Why not?" He grinned at me. "There aren't any heads of lettuce in her play. But there's a part that would be perfect for you."

"Is she a klutz, too?"

"Will you stop calling yourself that!"

"I'm only repeating what your dear friend Spud calls me."

"You don't have to believe everything anybody says."

"Then why should I believe you about being in a play?"

Andy gave me a sideways look. "Chris is going to try out," he said casually.

"Oh. . .?"

The curtain falls, and the audience breaks into thunderous applause. Chris takes my hand, and we step in front of the curtain to take our bows. Chris hands me a huge bouquet of red roses. . . .

"So, what do you say?"

"I have to think about it."

Maybe acting is my special talent, I thought. Maybe it's something I can do well. After all, didn't Andy say it was just like daydreaming?

Open the envelope, please. The award for best actress of the year goes to—Megan Steele!

Three

EARLY the next morning I climbed out of bed before anyone else was up. I slipped into an old pair of white shorts and a T-shirt, grabbed a bowl of cereal and a piece of toast, and hurried out to the workroom. I wanted to finish Mrs. Simpson's necklace.

I like jewelry. Mom made me a turquoise and lapis lazuli necklace last year for my birthday. Somehow, I managed to get the necklace caught on the handle of the water fountain at school when I leaned over to get a drink. There I was with my foot on the pedal that controls the water. I was bent over and water was spraying me in the face. . . . I don't wear necklaces or chains anymore.

Mom doesn't open the shop until nine, and she and Trish never come out to the workroom until after eight-thirty. After I finished Mrs. Simpson's necklace, I got out my acrylic paints and a rock I had cut and polished. I never know ahead of time what kind of a little creature I'm going to paint. They don't look like real animals, but I think they're kind of cute. They make me feel good when I look at them. Today, the creature turned out to be something like a combination of a two-humped camel and a hippopotamus. I called him Guthrie. That was the name of Dad's first puppy when he was a kid.

I wish I could paint like my father. He's not really famous yet, but everyone says he will be some day. I don't understand parents. How can a man and wife be in love one day and not the next? Mom and Dad kept telling me over and over that their divorce had nothing to do with Trish and me. But I don't know. . . . I hate to think about the divorce. I shoved the thoughts about my dad in that same little cubbyhole in my mind where I put all the unpleasant and embarrassing things in my life. I'm only fourteen, and already that cubbyhole's pretty full.

I was almost finished with Guthrie when I heard Mom and Trish out front. Quickly, I put my things under the counter. I got them out of sight just as Mom and Trish walked in.

"You're up early," Mom said. "Good, I see you finished the necklace." She examined it carefully. "It looks fine, dear. You did a good job."

I always get this nice warm tingle on my neck when anybody praises me. I perked up a bit after that.

Mom gave both Trish and me a new job. I had to repair the corner on an ornate gold frame that a customer had knicked. Trish was supposed to restring a necklace she had botched.

"Mom, can I do it later?" Trish asked. "Barrett's got in some new evening gowns. I want to look for one for the contest."

"You can go this afternoon. Do the necklace first."

"The pretty ones will be sold," Trish muttered.

All Trish ever talks about is the contest. I'll be so glad when Festival Week is over.

"I'm going into the studio for a while," Mom said. "You girls watch the shop."

We have a big room on the north side of the building where Mom sculpts. As she started for the studio, the front bell jangled. A high voice called, "Anybody here?"

I looked out through the entranceway to the shop. Oh, no, I thought, Mrs. Rhodes and Chris! I'd completely forgotten they were coming in to look at Dad's paintings.

I ducked down out of sight.

"What's the matter with you?" Trish asked.

"Nothing," I whispered. The hot flood of embarrassment hit me again, and I wanted to crawl into a hole. "I just don't want Chris Rhodes to see me."

"Well, I don't blame you. You look terrible. Why in the world do you wear that silly ponytail? And put on some eye makeup, Megan. Your face looks about as interesting as an undercooked pancake."

"Thanks," I hissed. "Not all of us can be Miss San Angelo."

Trish was looking out through the opening. "Chris is really cute. I wish he were a few years older."

I peered out, too. Chris was all dressed in white again—white shorts, white shirt, and V-necked sweater. How does he get his clothes so white? I wondered. I glanced down at my own white shorts. They looked pinkish-gray. Of course that's probably because I washed them with a red sweater last month.

We could hear Mom, Chris, and his mother talking about Dad's pictures.

"Christopher, do you like this one?" Mrs. Rhodes was measuring a landscape painting with a metal tape. "I don't much care for mountains, but it's just the right size. And the color is good for the dining room."

"It's okay," Chris said.

"Okay!" I whispered to Trish. "Okay? That's one of Dad's best paintings!"

"I think I'll take these four largest pictures if you can deliver them this morning," Mrs. Rhodes said. "I want to be sure they fit before we have our open house. Of course later, I may decide to change the frames."

"I'll bring them up right away," Mom said. I could tell by the tone of her voice that she was ticked off, too. "If they aren't satisfactory, you may certainly return them."

While Chris's mother wrote out a check, Chris moved closer to the workroom. He was looking at the case of jewelry. I ducked down out of sight. After a bit, my leg went to sleep. What was I doing hiding back here? I thought disgustedly. Was I going to hide in a burrow like some scared rabbit? I decided right then I'd try out for the play. Maybe Andy was right. Acting might help me get over being a klutz.

* * * * *

At ten I get to take an hour break. I usually run over to the Pizza Palace. But after yesterday, I decided to stay home. I should have known Carla and Helen Mae would stop by.

"We thought you might be too embarrassed to show your face at the Palace," Carla said.

She was never going to let me forget that disaster.

We went out to the kitchen for something to drink. Helen Mae and Carla perched on the high bar stools at the counter while I looked in the fridge. "The only thing diet we have is root beer."

"I really prefer lemon-lime," Carla said, "but root beer's better than nothing."

"Do you have any ice cream to put in it?" Helen Mae asked. "I love floats."

Carla looked at her in disgust. But amazingly, she didn't say anything. I guess she's tired of warning Helen Mae about her weight.

"Sorry," I said. "Trish won't allow any ice cream or goodies in the house until after the Miss San Angelo contest."

Then I knew why Carla wasn't picking on Helen Mae. She was after me.

"Well, you certainly blew it yesterday with Chris," Carla said. "I tried to tell Christopher not to be angry at you, that you're just accident prone."

"You didn't need to tell him anything," I said coldly.

"Actually, we didn't even talk about you. He's

such an interesting pers—"

"Oh, knock it off, Carla," Helen Mae broke in. "You didn't talk to him more than thirty seconds."

Carla tossed her head in that way of hers. It reminds me of a horse brushing off flies.

"You can learn a lot about someone from just a brief moment," she said loftily.

"Let's drop the subject," I said. Angrily, I threw my root beer can into the trash. I missed and hit the wall. The can wasn't empty, and brownish foam spewed everywhere. With a long-suffering sigh, I yanked a paper towel from the holder. The entire roll came off and knocked the butter dish off the counter, splatting soft butter onto the newly-scrubbed tile floor.

"My gosh," Carla said in an awed voice, "you're a regular one-woman disaster area. The Red Cross should follow you around."

"Leave her alone," Helen Mae said, and began to clean up the mess. "She can't beat my little brother. When you feed him, he blows his baby food everywhere. Have you ever cleaned spinach and liver off the walls?"

I slumped down in the middle of the kitchen. "What's the use!" I wailed. "I can't do anything right."

Helen Mae sat down on the floor beside me

and put her arm around me. "It's okay. It's okay," she said soothingly. I guess she's used to comforting her little brothers and sisters.

As if I normally carried on a conversation sitting in the middle of the kitchen floor, Carla went on chattering. "Did you hear the latest news? The Rhodes are having an open house at the mansion a week from Sunday. It's going to be catered by Mr. Yokomura."

"I hope he doesn't serve his octopus pizza," I said sourly. "I suppose they invited the whole town."

"Nope. Just the business and professional people—and their families." Carla chortled. "That means us. We'll be invited."

So who cares? I thought. I wasn't going within ten miles of Christopher Rhodes.

While Carla and Helen Mae were talking about the open house, I finished cleaning up the mess.

"I wonder what I should wear?" Carla was saying. "A dress, probably. Maybe Daddy will spring for a new outfit."

"The only decent thing I have is my Christmas dress," Helen Mae said, "if it still fits."

"It seems like a person should wear a ball gown to a mansion," I said as I swept up the last of the root beer and butter mess. I held the broom to my chest and closed my eyes.

A carriage drawn by six white horses is pulling up. A young woman is stepping out onto a red carpet. She is gorgeous with golden blond hair, golden skin, and a gown of shimmering gold.

The prince greets her and leads her into the ballroom. He takes her in his arms. They are the perfect couple—Golden Girl and Prince Charming . . .

"Now, what are you dreaming about," Carla said sarcastically, "that you're Cinderella going to the ball?"

My face flushed at how close she'd come to what I was thinking.

"Who is he?" Carla pressed. "If it's Chris Rhodes, you can forget it."

Ever since I was a little kid I've loved fairy tales. I often have these daydreams about a handsome prince. The trouble is, I can never quite see his face.

I quickly changed the subject. "Helen Mae, are you still going to try out for the play Andy's mom is putting on for Festival Week?"

"I don't know. Do you think I should?"

"Why not?" I said. "I'm thinking about it, too."

Both of them just stared at me.

"Now, I've heard everything," Carla said,

shaking her head. "You can't even give a book report in front of the class without causing a disaster."

I glared at her. "Just because I loused up once doesn't mean I'll do it again."

She was talking about the time I gave a book report on a mystery story. I was really into it, making it really scary. Near the end, the killer was climbing up the stairs, coming after the heroine. I lowered my voice, and every kid in the class leaned forward. "The killer was coming closer and closer. The heroine's heart hammered. The blood pounded in her head. The stairs squeaked. She drew back against the wall and held her breath. The door slowly opened. . . ." As I said the words I drew my arm back as if I were opening the door and my elbow hit the radiator. I let out a howl. The whole class screamed.

I got an *F* on my report because the teacher thought I did it on purpose to scare everybody.

Andy was right about one thing, though. While I'd been telling the story, I'd forgotten about myself. I hadn't been nervous or anything.

"I am going to try out," I said firmly. "I probably won't get a part anyway."

"We have a good chance," Helen Mae said. "All the juniors and seniors will be working on the carnival."

"Chris will be trying out for the play," I said casually.

Carla practically jumped off the stool. "How do you know he's trying out?"

"Andy told me," I said, happy that for once I knew something she didn't.

"Oh. . .well, I suppose it might be kind of fun to be in a play. As long as you guys are going, I'll come along to keep you company."

I've heard that if you count to ten you won't say something you might be sorry for later.

I counted to 387 . . . slowly.

Four

Just as Carla had said, Mrs. Rhodes invited all the business and professional people and their families to the open house. Carla's dad is the mayor, but he also owns Townsend's Cleaners. Andy's dad is in real estate, Spud's folks run the motel next door, and Helen Mae's family owns a little antique shop. That meant my friends and I were invited.

The open house was from one o'clock to four. Mom and Trish decided to go at one, but all of the kids had planned to leave about an hour later. Helen Mae's brother Ernie was the only one with a car. He was supposed to pick me up at a quarter till three.

I carefully dressed in my white cotton Easter outfit. I polished my white sandals and spilled only a tiny bit of polish on the bathroom floor.

Although my stomach felt empty, I was too nervous to eat lunch. I wanted so badly to make a good impression on Chris. But when I'm nervous, terrible things happen. I remember the time we went to San Francisco for an awards dinner honoring my dad. I still shudder whenever I think about it.

Dad, Mom, Trish, and I got all dressed up to go to this super fancy hotel banquet room. I managed to get through the meal without any problems. We were seated at the head table. The waiter cleared everything but the water glasses, coffee cups, and one pesky fly that kept landing on the table.

I was getting more and more nervous. Some big shot in the art world was introducing Dad and his family. I whispered to Mom, "Do we have to say anything or just stand up and smile?" She shushed me.

My mouth was dry. I drank most of my water. Then I worried that I'd have to go to the bathroom. Suddenly the fly landed right in front of me. To this day I don't know how I could have done it. But without thinking, I slammed my glass on the fly. The fly smashed all over the white linen cloth just as I heard, ". . . our honored guest, Malcolm Steele."

I'm surprised Dad didn't divorce us right there and then.

I shoved that disaster out of my mind and went out to the workroom to paint on my rocks. Sometimes it takes my mind off things. I got out my red acrylic paint and started a new little critter. It was part gremlin, and part anteater. When I'm painting, I always get so involved that I forget everything. The telephone's shrill ring startled me. My hand jerked and hit the bottle of paint. It splashed on the worktable and dripped onto the tile floor. With one hand, I grabbed the phone. With the other I was frantically trying to mop up the mess.

"Hello," I cried, "I can't talk now." I started to hang up but heard Spud yelling.

"Megan! Listen. We're picking you up in fifteen minutes. Be ready."

He didn't give me a chance to answer. Quickly, I swabbed up the floor and table, but then I noticed the red splatters all over my white cotton dress. Mom was going to kill me. I ran to the bathroom, yanked off the dress, and put it to soak in the sink.

I looked through my closet, pulling things off hangers. The only decent dress that fit anymore had a torn hem that I'd forgotten to mend. "Absolutely do not show up in jeans or shorts," Mom had said. "You wear a dress."

There wasn't time to sew up the hem, so I

rushed into Trish's room. She'd let me borrow her clothes before. I figured she wouldn't mind in an emergency.

You should see her closet. It's disgusting. Everything's so neat. I grabbed the first summery-looking dress I saw and slipped it on.

Trish and I are about the same size. I'm taller, but she fills out the tops better. I didn't remember having seen the dress before. It was pretty—greenish turquoise with spaghetti straps, a full skirt, and a short jacket. On the hanger was a shell necklace that Trish had made. I put it on to help cover the low neckline.

My white sandals looked okay with the dress. Luckily I hadn't spilled paint on them.

A car honked out front.

I glanced in the mirror. Not bad, I thought. In fact, I looked pretty good—and at least a year older. In this outfit, I ought to make an impression on Chris.

I dashed out front and stumbled over a rock, but I managed to catch my balance. Spud opened the door of the old station wagon, and called, "Watch out, everybody, here comes Megan the Klutz!"

Ernie, his girlfriend Gloria, and Spud were in the front seat. Carla and Helen Mae were in the back. "Hi, all," I said as I climbed in beside Carla.

"Watch it," she cried. "You're sitting on my dress. You'll wrinkle it."

"Sorry." I say that word a lot. "Where's Andy?" I asked.

Spud turned around and leaned over the seat. "He has to help Mr. Yokomura take more food up to the mansion. I sure hope there's some left when we get there."

Spud eats enough for six people, but he's skinny. I was surprised he wasn't feeding his face right now.

Helen Mae leaned around Carla to look at me. "Hey, when did you get the new dress? I love it."

"It's nice," Carla said in a lukewarm tone of voice. "But it's more your sister's color than yours."

"It is Trish's dress. I spilled paint on mine, so I borrowed hers."

Spud raised his eyes to the roof. "So what else is new?"

"You both look great," I said generously. Although I really thought Helen Mae was overdressed. She had on a shiny purple jersey that clung to her bulges like skin.

"I couldn't get into my Christmas dress," Helen Mae said. "I had to wear this hand-me-down of my aunt's. I look awful," she moaned, "like a huge purple eggplant."

Nobody argued with her.

Carla looked cute in a pink and white sundress. I think she could wear a laundry bag and still look cute.

It was only a short drive up Enright Hill to the mansion. It was built back in the thirties by a retired movie producer. It's all pink stucco, arches, and red tile roofs, the kind of place you see in pictures of Hollywood.

We all piled out of the car and headed for the house. My hands began to feel damp. *Please don't let me do something dumb,* I prayed. *Let me make a good impression on Chris this time.*

Mrs. Rhodes met us at the door. "Come in. I'm so glad you could make it," she said. But I could tell by her glazed look that she wasn't even sure who we were. She nodded toward a huge banquet room filled with long tables loaded with food. "Help yourselves."

Before Spud could zero in on the food, Chris came up to us.

He looked wonderful. He was wearing white again—white pants and a white shirt with a blue blazer. My insides felt like a bowl of Jell-o dessert that had been in the sun too long. I looked everywhere but at his face.

"Hi, everybody," he said.

I peered up through my lashes to find him looking at me. "Aren't you the girl who—"

"Yeah," I finished for him. "I'm the one. Do you want me to leave?"

"No. It wasn't your fault."

"Maybe not," Spud said with an evil grin. "But you'd better watch out, Chris. Megan the Klutz will get you."

Chris laughed. "I'll take my chances. Come on. If you want to see the place, I'll show you around."

Carla got as close to Chris as she could and began gushing about how wonderful the house was. The place was fabulous, all right. The huge living room had a Spanish look. It was filled with carved, ornate furniture and wooden chandeliers suspended from high ceilings. And there was actually a fountain in the center of the room.

As we walked on through the mansion, our shoes clicked loudly on the mosaic tile floor. Chris took us outside to show us the tennis court, the pool, and the rest of the beautifully-landscaped grounds.

We ended up back in the dining room where we found Andy wearing a white jacket. He was helping Mr. Yokomura set huge bowls of potato salad, fruit salad, and shell macaroni and shrimp salad around platters of fresh fruit, turkey and ham, and cheeses. To tell you the truth I was kind of disappointed. I had expected Mrs. Rhodes to serve caviar, little bitty sandwiches, and all that fancy stuff. I was starving though, so anything looked good.

"Come on, everybody," Chris said. "Please help yourself to the food."

Spud and Helen Mae were filling their plates as if they hadn't eaten for a month.

"Here, Megan," Andy said as he held out a plate. He had arranged it with slices of turkey, ham, mangoes, pineapple, and green, orange, and red melons. It looked wonderful. And right on top was the reddest, most luscious-looking strawberry I'd ever seen.

"Thanks, Andy." I looked around for tables or at least a chair. "Where do we eat?"

"Anyplace." He handed me a glass of fruit punch.

"You mean I have to try to balance this plate and glass, and try to eat at the same time?"

"You do it like this," Chris said. He put the glass and the plate in his left hand. But when I tried it the glass started to slip. "Here, let me help—" he began.

"No! Don't get near me," I cried.

He didn't listen to my warning. As he took

48

the glass from me, his hand bumped my plate. The plate tilted.

"Watch out!" Carla yelled.

The huge red strawberry slid slowly toward Chris. Just as it catapulted off the edge of the plate, I made a frantic grab with my right hand.

Have you ever had a handful of mooshy, dripping strawberry? I can tell you, it's totally disgusting. My face must have been as red as the berry. All I wanted to do was to go home before I did something really gross.

"Great catch," Chris said. "Are you on the softball team?"

"No," I mumbled. "People never want me on their side."

Andy handed me a damp cloth and whispered, "Don't let this throw you, Megan. At least Chris knows who you are."

"You're wearing my new dress!" Trish's shrill voice cut through the room. "That's for the contest!"

Suddenly it seemed as if everyone in town was in the dining room. I just stood there, my face burning. Did she have to make a big deal out of it in front of Chris? Nervously, I twisted the shell necklace. I heard a snap and shells flew everywhere—on the table, on the floor, down the front of the dress.

"Now, look what you've done!" Trish shrieked.

"The klutz strikes again," Spud said.

"Megan, I think you'd better come home with Trish and me," my mother said quietly.

"In a minute. I have to pick up these shells."

Partly to hide my embarrassment, I crawled under the table to search for shells. Shells? Oh, no, I thought. Shell macaroni. With my luck . . . I raised up just in time to see Chris take a bite of the macaroni and shrimp salad.

"No!" I cried. "Don't—"

But it was too late. He bit down on a shell and howled, "I think I've broken a tooth!"

I wished I could disappear from the face of the earth. Chris would never forgive me now. Oh, I'd made a great impression on him, all right. In fact, every boy I knew would run the other way when he saw me coming. Well, who needed boys, anyhow?

Yes, Mother Superior, I've decided to become a nun. I never want anything to do with boys again. Ever.

Five

THE next day I was still so upset that Mom let me take the day off after I repaired Trish's necklace.

Frankly, I thought the broken necklace was Trish's fault. If she'd done a good job on it in the first place, it never would have broken so easily. Naturally I didn't tell Trish that. All the way home from the open house, she had gone on and on about my wearing her dress. She kept bringing up things I'd done in the first grade, for gosh sakes.

As soon as I finished the repair job, I headed over to Helen Mae's house. It's a big, old place that looks about ready to fall down. It's neat, though. It has all these turrets and gables and funny-shaped rooms. When we were little, Helen Mae and I used to think there were secret rooms and hidden passages. The antique shop is in the parlor. Carla calls it a secondhand store. It's the only place in the house where kids aren't allowed.

I clanged the brass bell on the front door, and about ten little kids came running to open it. There's always a big gang of little kids at Helen Mae's house. I never have figured out where they all come from. The Vorcheks only have six.

"Helen Mae's in the kitchen," her five-year-old brother Jimmy told me. "She's making fudge."

I could smell the rich, chocolaty scent clear out in the entryway. Piano music drifted in from the living room. Mr. Vorchek gives piano lessons. I took lessons from him a couple of years ago, but playing the piano is not one of my talents, either.

Mrs. Vorchek was in the parlor with a customer. She waved as I passed the door. I like Helen Mae's mom and dad a lot. They always make you feel like you're part of the family. Maybe that's why there are always so many neighbor kids hanging around.

Jimmy and his friends dragged me out to the huge old-fashioned kitchen with a fireplace in it. I tripped over a little toy car and banged my ankle on a tricycle pedal. The place is always full of playpens, highchairs, strollers and stuff for kids.

"Hi, Megan," Helen Mae said. "I'll be right with you as soon as I finish this."

She was pouring a huge kettle of hot fudge out onto a slab of marble.

"I want to lick the pan," a chorus of little voices piped.

Me, too, I wanted to say. The chocolate smell was making my mouth water.

"Everybody on the floor in a circle," Helen Mae said as she passed out spoons. "Careful, the pan might be hot."

I love to come to Helen Mae's house. The Vorcheks are pretty poor, I guess. Helen Mae never has any money, but nobody seems to mind. The place is always full of people and laughter. I feel comfortable—you know?

"Are you baby-sitting?" I asked.

"No. You know me. When I feel crummy, I like to make fudge."

I eat ice cream—when Trish isn't on a diet. But a pound of fudge would do in a pinch. "What's wrong?" I asked.

She ran her finger along the edge of the soft candy until she had a huge glob, then shoved it into her mouth. "Me. Everything. I'm hopeless. I'll probably never have a date or be kissed by a guy. . ."

Maybe we should both become nuns, I thought.

"Me, too," I said. "But at least you didn't make a fool of yourself like I did yesterday. Did Chris break a tooth?"

"No, but he was really upset for a while. Here," she said sympathetically, "have some fudge."

She handed me a tablespoon, and we both dug into the candy. "What happened after I left yesterday?" I asked.

"Chris invited a bunch of us to go skating after the open house. We tried to call you, but your mom said you'd gone to bed."

I'd locked myself in my room, but I sure hadn't slept. "I suppose Carla made a big play for Chris? Did she wear that cute new skating outfit?"

"She did both, but Chris—oh, Megan, you'll never believe it—Chris skated with me two or three times."

"Well, why not? You're a good skater. So, what are you complaining about?"

"Because with me, all he talked about was skating. When he was with Carla, they were laughing and joking. He didn't even look at me as if I were a girl." She took another spoonful of candy. "It's too depressing to even think about."

The kids had finished with the pan. Helen Mae cut the fudge into pieces. "Now,

54

everybody that doesn't live here, go on home."

She told her own brothers and sisters to play in the backyard for a while. She amazes me how she never gets upset with the kids or yells at them. Trish and I are always arguing.

"Have another piece of fudge," she told me. "Then let's go to my room where we can talk."

I looked at the slab of fudge. Suddenly it didn't look so good. When we make fudge at home we grease the plate with butter or margarine. Helen Mae, to save money, I guess, had used shortening.

"No, thanks," I said. "I'm trying to cut down on sweets."

She put the pan and spoons to soak, then we went on upstairs to her room on the top floor. It's small, and the roof slants on one side so you have to stoop over or bump your head. She has it to herself. But even up here there's no privacy. Once I slept over. I was on the cot nearest the door. I woke up to find a strange little kid standing there staring at me. I reared up and whispered, "Boo." He took off like a scared rabbit. I never have seen the kid again.

We both stretched out on the cots on our stomachs. Helen Mae raised up on one elbow. "You know," she said, "I think it's my name. I'll bet if I changed my name I'd be more popular. I mean, who's going to look at a person named Helen Mae? It's so old fashioned and frumpy."

I thought about that for a bit. I didn't really think that changing her name would help, but if it would make her feel better, then I was all for it. "Sure," I said, "it's a good idea. Do you have a name picked out?"

"Well, I kind of like Mitzi or Trixie. Or how about Poppy? Those names sound perky and cute, like somebody who'd be fun. What do you think?"

"Yeah, I guess. But is that the image you want? How about something really sophisticated like—Celeste or Deirdre or Felicia?"

"Felicia Vorchek—not bad." Helen Mae jumped up from the cot and paraded around the room. She held out her hand and said haughtily, "My deah, deah Megan, please call me Felicia."

I giggled. "I'm not sure you're the Felicia type, either. Anyway, how would you get people to call you that? Why don't you just cut off the Mae and change the first part to Helena?"

She plunked down on the bed. "That's a super idea. Helena. From now on I'm Helena Vorchek."

"Helen Mae!" a voice yelled from downstairs. "Telephone."

We looked at each other and grinned. "Maybe it's a guy," she said. "Gosh, do you think the change of name is working already?"

I went down with her. But it was only Carla on the phone. I got up close so I could hear, too.

"Is Megan there?" Carla asked.

"I'm here," I said into the phone.

"Are you two going to the tryouts this afternoon?"

I'd completely forgotten about the play.

"Just a minute," Helen Mae said, then put her hand over the mouthpiece. "Do you want to go?"

I shrugged. "I don't know. Do you?"

"I guess it wouldn't hurt to go and watch," Helen Mae whispered. "We don't have to try out for a part if we don't want to."

"Carla, are you going?" I asked into the phone.

"Of course. Chris and I will be there."

Helen Mae and I looked at each other, then we both spoke at once. "We'll be there, too."

* * * * *

When we walked into the high school auditorium where Mrs. Gerritson was holding the tryouts, I changed my mind.

"I'm leaving," I told Helen Mae.

"Please stay. You don't have to try out. But I won't be so nervous if I know you're here."

"Oh, all right." I guessed it wouldn't hurt me to watch. "I'll wait for you."

Andy's mom had placed a lot of chairs in a circle near the stage. She was passing out playbooks to the kids. She puts on all the plays and pageants in town. Andy says she used to be an actress and a director before he was born. She worked in movies and even had a part in a Broadway play in New York. I love her voice. And I like the way she dresses. She always wears caftans and long earrings.

I found a seat in the third row of chairs where I could hear but where no one would notice me.

Only someone did—Andy.

"Hi, Megan. Glad you showed up. I called your place to remind you, but your sister said you weren't home."

"I was over at Helen Mae's," I said. "I just came along to keep her company."

"You're going to try out, aren't you?"

"No way. Not me. Absolutely not."

"Sure you are." He grabbed my hand and pulled me up. "Come on, they'll be starting in a minute."

I glared at him. "I don't want to be in a play.

Remember Letty Lettuce?" I asked.

He practically dragged me up to the group, sat me in a chair next to Chris, and handed me a playbook. I glanced over at Chris and gave him a sickly smile. I wished I were anyplace else—maybe on Mars.

There were eleven in the circle. "I'm Mrs. Gerritson," Andy's mom said. "But call me Mrs. G. It's easier." Then she went around the circle introducing each of us. When she got to Helen Mae, Helen Mae contradicted her. "My name is Helena Vorcheck."

Spud snickered. Carla stared at Helen Mae as if she were crazy. Chris looked amused.

Mrs. G went quickly on to the next person. "Open your books to the first scene of the first act," she said.

The blurb on the playbook said it was a three-act comedy about a ghost. During a seance, a medium contacts the ghost, and the ghost returns to his home. There were parts for eight people. The others would help out backstage—with the production, and with costumes and makeup.

Mrs. G asked different kids to read the parts. Some of them couldn't get out one line without breaking up. Carla and Chris read the leads. Then Chris and I read. Spud and Helen Mae were awful. He kept laughing, and she was so nervous she could hardly get the words out. I read several parts, including Mrs. Palmeteer, the medium. Another girl had read it first and had clowned it up. I started out that way, but as I got more into the scene, I read the lines seriously. I could really get into this poor lady who believed she could talk to the dead. The more seriously I said the lines, the more the kids laughed.

I finished the scene, and I nearly fell off my chair when the kids started clapping. "That was very good," Mrs. G said. "Did you read the play ahead of time?"

"No," I said. "I've never heard of it before."

"All right, everyone," Mrs. G said. "Why don't you take a fifteen-minute break. When you get back, I'll hand out the parts."

As we started out, Andy stopped me. "Didn't I tell you you'd be good? I could tell Mom was impressed. It's hard to find good character actors."

"Andy?" his mom called. "Could you help me over here?"

"See you later, Megan. I have to go."

I hurried outside to join the other kids. They were trying to guess who would get the parts. The only one that everybody agreed on was Chris. We all thought it was a cinch that he'd get the part of the ghost.

"It's just that I've been in a lot of plays before," Chris said modestly.

"Chris," I said quietly, so no one else could hear me. "I'm sorry about your tooth."

"It's fine. I'm just sorry you left in such a hurry. You could have gone skating with us." He stopped and grinned. "Maybe not—you could destroy a skating rink."

"I could destroy a padded cell."

He glanced at his watch. "It's time. Good luck, everybody."

Helen Mae walked back with me. "Isn't he wonderful? I'd give the world to play the lead opposite him. But I was awful."

"It wasn't as scary as I thought it would be," I said. "Even if I don't get a part, I'm glad I tried out."

We joined the others in the circle. As everybody had expected, Chris got the male lead. "Carla," Mrs. G said, "I'd like you to play the widow."

Carla squealed. "Oh, Mrs. G, you won't be sorry. Thank you, thank you," she gushed.

Mrs. G gave out the other parts. Finally, she came to Sophia Palmeteer, the medium. I closed my eyes and held my breath.

"Megan Steele, I'd like you to play the medium." Mrs. G held out a playbook with my name on it.

I took it with trembling fingers. I'm going to be in a play, I thought. From now on I'll never be self-conscious any more. I'll never do any more dumb things because I'm nervous. Never again will I be a klutz.

Six

CARLA, Helen Mae, and I went to our first rehearsal the next evening. When I'd learned that I'd play the medium, I had been too dazed to realize that neither Spud nor Helen Mae had gotten a part. Mrs. G asked them both to help with props. And they were both prompters, so they had to go to every rehearsal.

I was so nervous, I forgot my playbook and had to go back home for it. Carla griped about that all the way to the auditorium.

"They'll probably think we're not coming, and Mrs. G will give my part to someone else," Carla said in her usual snippy way.

"Don't be silly," I said. "We're only a couple of minutes late."

"Well, I don't see how you're going to remember your lines if you can't even remember to bring the playbook," Carla said.

"You'll probably ruin the play."

She was probably right. This idea of Andy's was crazy. What if I forgot my lines and just stood there with my mouth hanging open? Not only would my friends know I was a fool, but so would the whole darned town. I sure wanted to show Carla, though. And it would be fun . . . if I weren't so scared. Oh, what's the use? I'd just be Letty Lettuce all over again. I decided to tell Andy I was backing out.

By the time we got to the auditorium, most of the cast was there. I hurried over to Andy. "I need to talk to you," I whispered.

"We're just about to start. Can it wait?"

"I guess so," I said.

He looked pleased with himself. "Aren't you glad now that you tried out?"

Before I could answer, his mom called, "All right, everybody, find a seat. We're just going to read through the play a couple of times before we go up on the stage."

There never seemed to be a good time to tell Mrs. G that I wanted out. And as we read through the play, I found I was actually enjoying it. In one scene we all got the giggles so badly that Mrs. G had to call a five-minute break.

Andy came over to me. "Now, what was it you wanted to tell me?"

"That your mom should get somebody else to play the medium. This was a dumb idea."

"You can't back out now. Nobody else read the part as well as you did."

"Yeah, I read it okay, but you know how I'm always forgetting things. I'll get up there in front of an audience and freeze."

"You're lucky it's only a small part," Carla said. I hadn't noticed that she and Chris had come up behind us. "What if you had to learn the lead?"

"After a while you'll know everybody's lines," Chris said. "But if you have trouble, I'll help you. You just need someone to cue you."

A warm feeling swept over me. Christopher Rhodes had offered to help me. I'd be crazy to quit now, I thought. I might never get a better chance to be alone with him.

"We have a couple of important scenes together," he added. "The practice would help me, too."

Boy, you should have seen Carla's face.

"You and I ought to rehearse together," she said to Chris. "After all, we're in practically all the same scenes."

"The four of us could get together," Andy said quickly. "I'm the assistant director. I know the way Mom wants everybody to say the lines."

I gave Andy a long look. He sounded almost—jealous. I'd never even guessed that he liked Carla. I should have known, though. She was the most popular girl in our class.

"You could use a couple of prompters, couldn't you? How about Helen Mae and me?" Spud asked. "We can make a party out of it."

"All right, everyone," Mrs. G. called. "Let's get back to work."

* * * * *

Two weeks later I was in the wings waiting for my cue and watching Carla walk through her part with a playbook in her hand. She still didn't know the first act. I was really surprised at how fast I learned my lines.

We were working with hand props and getting used to where the furniture would be. Even though there was no set yet, Andy had marked where all the doors would be with chalk on the floor of the stage. That was so we'd know where to make our entrances and exits. He also made marks for windows, mirrors, and big pieces of furniture like the piano and couch.

The night before, the six of us had gotten together to go over lines. Chris was really helpful to all of us. I thought he would be conceited, but he wasn't. You'd never know his parents were rich and that he'd been to France and England and had even gone on a safari to Africa.

A lion roars. He's getting closer and closer. I know it is my last moment on earth. Then I hear someone shout my name. A tanned, muscular figure comes swinging down on a vine. "I'll save you," he says. And he sweeps me up in his arms just as the lion reaches for me.

"Oh, Megan, I thought I had lost you," he says.

I look up, trying to see his face . . . .

"Megan! You're on!" It was Helen Mae.

I'd missed my cue. I rushed onto the stage. "Good after—" I began.

"Megan," Mrs. G called from the front row where she was watching, "you just walked through the window and trampled over the piano."

Everybody laughed.

"I'm sorry. I missed my cue and—"

"We'll take a short break and try it again," Mrs. G said patiently. "Only next time, try using the door."

"Megan never gets anything right," Spud said. "One time, instead of getting on the transit bus to go over to Riverview, she got on the bus with the boys' basketball team."

That had been one of my most embarrassing moments. I hadn't even noticed I was on the wrong bus for several minutes. I figured it out when I heard the guys snickering and making jokes.

"Hey, Spud," Andy said. "Megan got on that bus on purpose."

I shot Andy a look of gratitude for coming to my rescue. "Sure," I said. "What better way to get fifteen guys all to myself?"

"Well, Megan, I just hope you didn't make that entrance through the window in order to get a laugh," Mrs. Gerritson said.

"Oh, no! I promise I'll be more careful."

*　*　*　*　*

During the next week, I really tried hard to do everything right. But it seemed as if the harder I tried, the more I did wrong. I knew Mrs. G was unhappy about it.

On Saturday Mrs. G stopped Helen Mae and me after rehearsal. "Megan, do you have time to come into the dressing room for a few minutes?"

I glanced at Helen Mae. "Can she come, too?"

"That's fine with me, but it's personal," Mrs. G said.

"Helen M—Helena knows everything about me," I said.

As we headed for the girls' dressing room, I was trying to figure out what she wanted to talk to me about. Was she going to ask me to drop out of the play, I wondered.

We sat on benches. Mrs. G didn't say anything for a minute, and I got even more nervous. "I know I've been messing up. Are you going to give my part to someone else?" I asked.

"No, dear, of course not. I just wondered why you tried out for the play. It seems so painful for you. Every time you come on stage, you look as if you're going to have a heart attack."

I stared down at my hands and realized they were clenched into fists. My fingernails were digging into my palms. "Andy—I mean, I had this crazy idea that being in a play would help me get over being a klutz. And if I weren't a klutz, then the boys would like me. Dumb, huh?"

"No, it's not dumb at all. Acting in a play certainly can help a person get over shyness and self-consciousness. But I think in your case it will take more than that."

I sighed. "I'm just plain hopeless."

Mrs. G smiled at me and shook her head.

"Nothing is hopeless. Megan, what do you want to be some day?"

I didn't even have to think about that answer. "I just want to have one talent. My entire family is loaded with talent—art, dancing, design. But I can't do anything."

"Being creative isn't the only kind of talent. It takes talent to be a good friend."

That didn't seem very important to me. "I want to be rich and famous and pretty. And I'd like to get through one whole day without a disaster."

"Do you like yourself, Megan?" Mrs. G asked quietly.

What a weird question, I thought. "I don't know. I wish I were more like my sister." I sighed again. "Or Carla. Or Helen Mae— Helena."

"Me!" Helen Mae practically squealed. "Me? Nobody in the whole, entire world wants to be like me."

"You both are bright and sensitive and attractive," Mrs. G said. "Come over here by the mirrors."

She sat us down in front of the dressing table mirrors. "All right, now. Helena, what do you see?"

Helen Mae scrunched her shoulders and gave me a sickly grin. "The blob. The creature from outer space. A female nerd."

Mrs. G turned my head so I had to face the mirror. "And what do you see?"

"A nothing—like one of my dad's watercolor paintings that's faded and smeared."

"Isn't that amazing," Mrs. G said. "It must be a magic mirror. That's not what I see at all."

I looked up at her. "What do you see?" I asked.

"I see two young, fresh, sweet faces."

"Sweet!" I moaned. "Who wants to look sweet?"

"Yeah," Helen Mae said. "We want to be glamorous and have boys fall all over themselves to be with us, and—"

"It's fine to dream—to want to be beautiful, popular, and famous. But if you don't like the person you are—the person deep down inside—then you'll probably never be very happy."

"Okay," I said, "but how do you learn to like yourself?"

"By not comparing yourself to your sister or to anyone else. Be the best 'you' that you can be. Make the best of your own looks and talents and mind."

"How?" I wanted to know. "I don't want to go to a charm school like Trish did."

"Charm schools offer a great deal of help. You can learn etiquette, poise, how to wear your makeup and hair, how to dress, and even how to talk to boys on the phone or on a date."

Helen Mae and I looked at each other. Trish had never mentioned that part about boys.

"Well," Helen Mae said, "it sounds good, but I can't afford anything like that."

"When I worked in Hollywood, I learned about most of those things. If you want, I'd be glad to help you both."

"Even with how to talk to boys?" Helen Mae asked.

"Let's deal with the other things first."

"When can we start?" I asked.

Mrs. G looked at her watch. "How about right now? I have an hour I can spare."

* * * * *

For the next week or so, Mrs. G worked with Helen Mae and me every chance she could. We learned how to breathe correctly, how to stand, how to walk with our knees flexed, how to use makeup, how to lower our voices and speak distinctly, how to wear our hair.

"Megan," she told me, "you should cover your hair when you're in the sun. Use a conditioner, and I'd suggest cutting your hair."

"Oh, I can't. My dad loves long . . . " I bit my lip. I never liked to talk about Dad in front of other people.

"I don't mean you should cut it short. Just get rid of the dead, split ends. Why don't you let me cut you some bangs and shorten the sides to soften your face."

"Okay," I said doubtfully.

Mrs. G got out her scissors. When she finished trimming my hair she asked, "How do you like it?"

I turned my head from side to side. "I don't know. I look different."

"You look great," Helen Mae said.

"You're lucky, Megan," Mrs. G said. "Your jaw line is excellent. You'll still look good at fifty."

I stuck out my chin and craned my neck. Nobody had ever mentioned my excellent jaw line. It reminded me to straighten my shoulders.

Mrs. G helped Helen Mae with diet and exercise. With me, she worked more on attitude.

"Forget about yourself, and think about the other person," she told me. "Stop worrying about what might happen. And if something bad does hap—"

"Oh, it will," I said. "It always does."

Mrs. G gave me a disgusted look. "So what if it does? It's not the end of the world. Remember, everyone goofs up sometimes. They just go on as if nothing had happened. They don't let things get them down. If you foul up, forget about it. Put it behind you."

I groaned. "But that's so hard."

"Nothing's easy. Give yourself permission to feel bad for a while, then put the situation out of your mind."

Everything Mrs. G said made sense. Helen Mae and I really tried to do what she had taught us. We practiced walking correctly, speaking better, and trying our best to be "charming."

Mom and Trish mentioned my new haircut, but they were both so busy with the pageant and Festival Week that they didn't notice much else. Even Carla was so wrapped up in the play that she didn't pay any attention to Helen Mae or me.

Andy sure noticed, though.

One evening after practice, he called to me. "Megan?"

I turned gracefully, flexed my knees, and walked over to where he was painting a scenery flat. "Yes?" I said in a deep, clear voice.

He wiped his hands on his pants—a nervous reaction, I thought—and looked at me closely. "What the heck are you doing to yourself lately?" he asked.

"What do you mean?" I asked, suddenly defensive.

"You look—great. Want to stop by the Pizza Palace and have a soda or something?" he asked.

"Thanks, but I have to get home. I'm supposed to finish a bracelet for Chris's mom."

"Oh . . . sure. Well, I should finish painting this flat before I leave, anyhow."

"See you tomorrow," I said. Andy didn't answer. He just hurried off to the storeroom.

On the steps in front of the auditorium, Chris was talking to Carla and some of the cast. When he saw me, he called, "Megan, wait up. I'm supposed to pick up a bracelet for my mother. If it's okay, I'll walk home with you."

I glanced at Carla. She looked ready to spit nails. "It's okay with me," I said. "But you'll have to wait for a bit. I still have to adjust the clasp."

Chris took my canvas bag. "See you at tomorrow's rehearsal," he said to the rest.

I managed a weak, "See you."

On the short walk to my place, I couldn't

think of anything to say. Oh, how I wished Mrs. G had told Helen Mae and me about how to talk to boys.

Luckily, Chris helped me out. I didn't have to say a word.

"This part of the ghost is the best one I've ever had," he said. "I can really relate to him."

I just nodded and put in a few *uh huhs* and *huh uhs.*

When we got home, Chris watched part of a baseball game while I finished the bracelet. I nearly fell over when he asked if I'd like to go over to the Pizza Palace for a hamburger. I just stood there like a dope.

"I didn't have much dinner," he said. "I'm starved."

I started to say, aren't you worried I'll spill catsup or mustard all over you? Then I remembered Mrs. Gerritson's words. *Forget about past mishaps. Put them all behind you.* With all the things I'd had to put behind me, I'd be afraid to ever look backwards again. "Okay," I said. "I'll just leave a note for Mom."

Going across to Yokomura's with Chris, I felt wonderful. It wasn't exactly a date, but it was the next best thing to it.

In the back booth we sit close together. He takes my hand and looks deep into my eyes.

"Megan, you are the most wonderful girl in the world . . . ."

I sighed. This time everything was going to go perfectly. I wasn't going to spill, rip, or mutilate anything.

But when we went inside, I saw Andy and Spud at the counter. I'd completely forgotten that Andy had asked me to have a soda with him. I moved to the far side of Chris and tried to shrink. I hoped Andy wouldn't see us.

"Let's take a back booth," I whispered.

"Oh, look, there's Andy and Spud." Before I could say anything, Chris called to them. "Why don't you guys join Megan and me?"

Andy turned slowly on the stool and gave me a long look. "Thanks, Chris, but I have to get home."

"Me, too," Spud said. Then he leered. "Boy, you're brave to come in here with Megan. She'll probably—"

"Knock it off, Spud," Andy said without even looking at me. "Come on, let's go."

I'd been so happy the minute before, but now I felt lousy. While we ate our hamburgers, Chris talked some more about the play and the part of the ghost. But all I could think about was Andy's face and the hurt look in his eyes.

For some reason, I wasn't nervous. I didn't

spill my drink or knock over the table or do one single klutzy thing.

Maybe being in the play and getting all the help from Mrs. G was working.

So, how come I didn't feel better about it?

Seven

THE five of us—Chris, Spud, Helen Mae, Carla, and I—practiced our lines together and usually went to rehearsals together. Andy had to go early to work on the set and to help his mom. Afterward, when it wasn't too late, Andy would join us at the Palace for pizza or sandwiches. He joked and kidded with everybody except me. Oh, he was polite, but I knew he was still upset with me.

Even Carla noticed that something was wrong. "What'd you do to Andy?" she asked one night when she and Helen Mae and I went to the restroom.

"I didn't do anything," I said sharply. "Well, I guess I did. But I don't see why he's so upset about it." I told her about refusing Andy, then later coming to the Palace with Chris. "It wasn't a real date. All we did was talk about the play." To tell the truth, I had been a little disappointed about that. "And, after all," I said, "Andy knows I like Chris a lot."

"You can forget about Chris," Carla said. "I'm going to get him to ask me for a date."

Helen Mae sighed. "You sure have the inside track, all right. You actually get to kiss him in the play."

"Yes, but Mrs. G won't let us practice the kiss until dress rehearsal." Carla grinned. "When we do, I wonder how many times I can get it wrong before she catches on?"

As I was combing my hair and fluffing out my bangs, Carla watched me in the mirror. Then she looked at Helen Mae and frowned.

"You two have been doing something different to yourselves. You look different."

Helen Mae and I both laughed. "We wondered how long it would take before you noticed," I said. "Andy's mom has been working with us—you know, giving us beauty tips and stuff."

"So how come you didn't let me in on it?" Carla demanded.

"Because you don't need any help," Helen Mae said.

Carla looked pleased at that. Then Helen Mae added, "But from now on, we're going to give you some competition with Chris."

"Oh really? You two are wasting your time."

With a pitying look at us, she swept out of the restroom.

Helen Mae made a growling sound. "Some day, I hope she gets what's coming to her. On opening night, maybe I'll put vinegar in her tea."

"Come on," I said. "Enough things happen by accident."

"I can dream, can't I?"

I knew Helen Mae would never do anything mean to anybody. Now, me—I just might.

* * * * *

Except for the few minutes before I had to make an entrance, I loved the rehearsals. I never could seem to get over being nervous. But the minute I stepped out on the stage as Mrs. Palmeteer, I was just fine.

In fact, I thought I was doing pretty well in the klutz department, too. I hadn't had a disaster in a couple of weeks. That was practically a record for me. But as we got closer to Festival Week, things started happening again.

One night we were going straight through the play without stopping.

"If anything goes wrong," Mrs. G said, "just pretend it's opening night, and carry on."

Right then I started to worry.

One of my best scenes came in the first act when Mrs. Palmeteer held a séance. Several characters and I were seated at a round table. The only light was from a dim lamp and the prompters' little penlights. My character, the medium, was to make contact with the ghost of Julian Fairhaven. I had to scream, and Spud had to turn the switch for the lamp at exactly the right second. In the dark, I was to come out of my trance under the table, as if I'd just slid out of my chair.

Everything was going fine. I contacted the ghost. Then I screamed and the lights went out. But somehow the table got knocked over. In the dark, I couldn't find it. I was crawling around on my hands and knees, frantically whispering to Helen Mae, "Where's the table? How can I get under it if I can't find it?"

Helen Mae shot the penlight right into my eyes.

"Watch it!" Someone yelled.

"Spud!" Mrs. G called. "Hit the lights! What in heaven's name is going on up there?"

The lights came on, and I nearly fainted for real. I had crawled right to the edge of the stage. "I'm sorry, Mrs. G, I got all turned around trying to find the table."

"It's all right. But next time, try to keep

going," she said patiently.

Oh, sure, I thought. If I'd kept going, I'd have fallen right off the stage and broken my stupid neck.

We started the scene again. I tried to remember Mrs. G's words. *If something bad happens, it's not the end of the world. Forget about it, and put it behind you.* Well, I tried, but I've had fourteen years of things going wrong. It's kind of hard to forget.

The second act took place in a park. We already had benches and some of the scenery set up. Andy had made a huge papier-mâché rock. It looked sturdy, so I wasn't particularly worried about having to climb up on it. I had to give one of my big speeches where I was trying to bring back the spirit of Julian.

I got my cue, jumped up on the rock, spread my arms, and began my lines. "By the mysteries of the deep, by the flames of banal, by the powers of the east . . . "

Suddenly, I heard a slight crackling noise. I continued my speech. "By the silence of the night . . . "

Another crackle.

In horror, I felt myself slowly, very slowly, begin to sink into the papier-mâché.

I heard a nervous titter. I slipped further into the rock. It was up past my ankles now.

Someone began to giggle, then people were laughing.

I skipped some of my lines to get to the important part. "I call thee by the ties of love," I said as fast as I could, almost shouting over the roars of laughter. "Spirit of Julian Fairhaven . . . "

"Stop!" Mrs. G yelled. But she was laughing, too. "Somebody help Megan out of there before she sinks up to her eyeballs."

Spud was laughing so hard he was holding his stomach.

"It wasn't my fault," I said, almost in tears.

Nobody heard me over the laughter.

On the entertainment scene tonight, Megan Steele sank into a rock, finding a new way to ruin a play. For an encore she will knock over a chair. The chair will hit a light and short out a circuit. That will start a fire and totally destroy the auditorium . . . .

I turned to look at Andy. He was grinning. Could he have sabotaged the rock?

No, it couldn't have been Andy. It was just another dumb accident.

* * * * *

The days just before Festival Week started were totally insane at my house. Mom was going nuts trying to get people to do their jobs. And Trish went around in a daze. The competition had been delayed for a couple of weeks because one of the contestants was sick. Trish was always practicing her walk or the song and dance number or what she'd say if she won. That left me with a lot of extra work in the shop.

The day before Festival Week began, it poured. I mean, we had thunder, lightning, and lots of wind. It was a regular cloudburst. Trish had a fit because that was the evening Miss San Angelo would be crowned.

"My hair is going to look awful!" she cried. "You know how limp it gets in damp weather." She glared at me as if I'd caused the storm. At dinner neither Trish nor I could eat a bite. My stomach was in a knot. But Trish was in even worse shape than I was. I'd never seen her so upset and nervous. She was yelling at everybody and everything. She sure wasn't going to win Miss Congeniality acting like that. Secretly, I couldn't help feeling a tiny bit glad that she had some of the same problems I did.

It was still storming when Mom and Trish were getting ready to leave for the Civic Auditorium. I couldn't go because we had a dress rehearsal that night.

I gave my sister a hug. "Good luck, Trish.

You look gorgeous," I told her.

"Thanks, Megan. Good luck to you tonight, too. Am I supposed to say 'break a leg'?"

"That's on opening night. And don't tell me that. You know me, I'd do it!"

As they left, Mom said, "Don't forget we have to help at the pancake breakfast in the morning. We're leaving at six."

"Six!" I cried.

"Six sharp," Mom said.

Next year, I hope somebody else will be the chairman of the Festival committee, I mumbled under my breath. Anything Mom can't get someone else to do, Trish and I get roped into doing. Take the parade tomorrow— guess who has to follow the horses with a cart and shovels?

It was too wet to walk to rehearsal, so Helen Mae called to say her brother would pick me up at six-thirty. I spent the time working on my rocks. Guthrie the Camelpotamus was still my favorite. So I painted Gertrude, a wife for him, and two little babies.

Helen Mae and her brother were late picking me up. One of the Vorchek kids had come down with chicken pox.

As I climbed into the backseat, I was surprised to see Chris.

"Chris had to return an antique," Helen

Mae said quickly. "His mom decided she didn't want it after all."

"I wish I could return my part in the play," I muttered. "I'm scared. My hands are already beginning to sweat."

"It's just a dress rehearsal," Chris said.

When we got to the auditorium, Helen Mae helped me with my costume. Mrs. Palmeteer was supposed to be a bit strange. I had to wear a long, flowing chiffon dress, several strings of beads, dangly earrings, and a fur around my neck that looked like two foxes biting each others' tails. Last came a horrible orange-red wig.

When I was dressed, Andy called to me. "Come on over here, and I'll make you up."

I had figured his mom would do everybody. But she was working on Chris, who was wearing a gray wig and was dressed all in gray. As Mrs. G applied gray makeup to his face, she asked, "Chris, are you all right? You look flushed, and your skin feels hot."

"I'm just tired, I guess."

I felt as if I had a fever, too. I sat down on one of the benches between Carla and Chris. Andy didn't say anything to me as he applied makeup base, lots of rouge and lipstick, and false eyelashes.

"Andy, are you sure Mrs. Palmeteer is

supposed to look like this?" I asked.

"Mom's orders," he said.

"Well, there's one good thing. If I ruin the play, nobody in the audience will know it's me. My own mother wouldn't recognize me."

"Are you nervous?" Andy asked me.

I was breathing too fast. My heart felt like it was pounding out an Indian war dance. "Nervous? Who, me? My knees always shake like this. Birds always flap their wings in my stomach."

"It's butterflies, not birds," Carla said from the bench next to mine.

"You have what you want in your stomach," I said. "I have birds."

I picked up my playbook and started going over my lines. The words blurred.

"Megan, take deep breaths," Andy said.

I took so many deep breaths in a row that I hyperventilated and nearly passed out. My throat was dry, and I thought I was going to throw up.

Andy handed me a paper cup of water from a thermos. "Drink this slowly, and calm down. You'll be fine as soon as you get on stage."

"Thanks," I said. "But I think you'd better tell your mom to find somebody to take my place. Helen Mae, you do it. Please." I started to pull off the wig.

"I don't know the lines," Helen Mae said.

"You can do it," Andy told me. "Just pretend you're really Mrs. Palmeteer."

"Ten minutes to curtain time," Mrs. G called.

"I'm going to be sick," I moaned. "I know it."

Megan Steele, star of stage, movies, and television, collapsed tonight during a performance of The Ghost Returns. *It is believed she suffered a heart attack . . . .*

"Megan, come on," Helen Mae said.

Andy and Helen Mae practically pushed me out to the wings where I was to make my first entrance. Helen Mae took her place on the prompter's stool. I peeked out through the curtain and nearly did have a heart attack.

"Who are all those people out there?" I whispered to Andy.

"Some of them are from the college. Mostly they're kids from Mom's drama classes. Then, there's a reviewer from the newspaper."

"A reviewer!" I squeaked. "I thought they came to opening night."

"They usually do, but Mom asked the one from the *San Angelo Sun* to come tonight. With a good review in tomorrow's paper, we might have a sellout for the whole week."

"I wish I'd never let you talk me into this,

Andy Gerritson. It was a stupid, dumb idea. I'm still a klutz. I'll always be a klutz."

Andy gave me a disgusted look. "Excuse me," he said. "I have to go work the lights."

Suddenly, recorded music began to play, and the curtain opened. I gave Helen Mae one last agonized look and waited for my cue—the door chimes.

A girl playing the servant escorted me inside where Carla, as Cecily Fairhaven, was seated at the piano. In this scene the widow asks Mrs. Palmeteer to try to contact her dead husband.

Carla sounded as stiff and scared as I felt, but we got through the scene all right. And at the end of the first act, we got a good hand from the people in the audience.

I was feeling pretty confident as I waited for Act Two to begin. As the curtain opened, I was alone on the stage waiting for Mrs. Fairhaven. I walked around the room for a moment and picked up a silver cigarette box as if contemplating stealing it. Then Carla was supposed to enter.

Only she didn't.

It seemed like hours passed as I stood there. Absently, I stuffed the silver box into my huge shopping bag. Then I walked around the room a few more times. What was I supposed to do next? Finally, I moved near Helen Mae and whispered, "For gosh sakes, where's Carla?"

"She got locked in the restroom," Helen Mae whispered back. "Ad-lib until they can get her out."

Ad-lib! Sure. I'm all by myself on the stage, and I'm supposed to make up lines. I was going to choke Carla when she did come on stage, and turn the play into a murder mystery.

There was a tea service on a silver tray. While I tried to think of something to say, I poured myself a cup of tea. Then I remembered Helen Mae's words, *maybe I'll spike the tea with vinegar.* I dropped the cup, knocked over the sugar bowl and all the little cubes scattered everywhere. As I got on my hands and knees to pick up the sugar cubes, the stupid fur got in my face. I was eyeball to eyeball with a dead fox. And it smelled like moth balls.

I heard a few snickers from the audience. I wanted to die right there. I wished there were a trap door in the stage that I could fall through.

Then I noticed that one of the sugar cubes had rolled under an end table. I got flat on my stomach, blew fur out of my face, and reached for the cube. I felt my hair catch on something and jerked back. I'd completely forgotten I was wearing a wig.

Now, I heard people laughing.

I slapped the wig back on my head just as Carla came running on to the stage. "Mrs. Palmeteer," she said in a rush, "I'm so sorry to keep you wait—for Pete's sake, what's happened to you?"

That definitely wasn't in the script. "Just a bit of an accident," I ad-libbed. I smoothed my dress, adjusted the furs, and patted my hair. It was only then that I realized the wig was on crooked. I must have looked like an idiot.

Somehow, we got through most of the scene until Carla was to pay me in advance for the séance. She looked around for the pen that should have been on the desk. "Where's the pen?" she cried. "It's supposed to be right here." I could see the panic in her face.

"I'm sure it must be around here someplace," I broke in and began to look around for it.

"In your bag," Helen Mae whispered.

In my bag? Suddenly I remembered putting things in it. "Perhaps you'd like to borrow mine," I said, fishing it out of the bag.

As I pulled out the cigarette case and other knickknacks, Carla's mouth fell open. The audience was snickering, and I realized they thought Mrs. Palmeteer had been stealing.

We finished the scene, but when we came

off, Carla ripped into me. "You did that on purpose, didn't you? I'll never forgive you for this, Megan Steele. You made me look unprofessional."

"I don't believe it. I make a total fool of myself and you worry about looking unprofessional," I said.

Carla glared at me and stormed off backstage.

The rest of the act went smoothly. The papier-mâché rock didn't give way. The séance table didn't fall off the stage. I didn't fall off the stage.

Everything went fine until the scene where the ghost shows up. Mrs. Palmeteer was the only one who was supposed to be able to see the ghost. Cecily asked me where he was. My line was, "He's over by the piano blowing his nose."

It came out, "He's over by the nose blowing his piano."

The audience roared. I wanted to sink back into the rock. As soon as the curtain closed, I ran off stage. But the laughter still rang in my ears.

Eight

EVERYBODY tried to tell me I had done just fine, but I wouldn't listen. I knew better. I'd ruined the play, and the critic from the *Sun* would give it a bad review. After the curtain call, I dashed backstage, tore off my costume, and rushed out without even taking off my makeup.

It was still raining, and by the time I got home I was soaked. I had hoped to arrive before Trish and Mom got back. But as I let myself in the kitchen door, I heard their happy, excited voices.

I swallowed hard, wiped my wet face with my sleeve, and walked slowly into the living room.

Trish was wearing her pretty beige lace evening gown. She had a wide satin ribbon across her shoulder, and a crown sparkled against her blond hair. I'd never seen her look so beautiful. She turned and saw me.

"Megan, guess what! I'm Miss San Angelo. Look!" She held out some envelopes. "I won a trip to New York, all expenses paid. And they gave me a $500 scholarship. The pageant was wonderful. I wasn't even scared."

Trish showed me her flowers, a plaque, and some other prizes.

I think Mom was as excited as Trish was. "I nearly went crazy," Mom said, "when they were announcing the runners-up."

Trish danced around the room. "I thought I was going to die right there on the stage."

"I knew you'd be crowned the queen," I said, and I meant it.

"I'm sorry you couldn't have been there—" Mom began. Then she stopped as she got a good look at me. "Megan, you're all wet. Didn't you get a ride home? Honey, you're a mess."

"You'd better get that makeup off," Trish said. "It's bad for your skin."

"How did dress rehearsal go?" Mom asked.

"Just great." Tears welled up in my eyes, and I turned away so they wouldn't know how upset I was. I didn't want to spoil Trish's celebration. I gulped back a sob. "I'd better get out of these wet clothes and go to bed," I said. "I'm really tired."

"That's a good idea," Mom said. "Don't forget, we all have to be up early."

I hurried to my room and flung myself on the bed. What a lousy, crummy night.

Would anything ever, ever go right for me?

* * * * *

The next morning was bright and sunny. My eyes were gritty and my face felt as if I hadn't gotten off all the makeup. All I wanted to do was to stay in bed forever so I wouldn't have to face everybody. The night before I'd had several phone calls, but I'd told Mom I was too tired to talk to anyone.

I came out to the kitchen where Mom and Trish were drinking coffee. Trish was still bubbling about being chosen Miss San Angelo. All that happiness made me feel worse. "Mom, may I please stay home?" I asked.

"No, you may not! You have a job to do. I've had enough of irresponsible people to last me a lifetime," Mom said. "The bakery just called to say they didn't think they had enough pies for the pie-eating contest. So could we use cakes? And the men didn't get the booths finished for the arts and crafts displays because it was too rainy yesterday!"

I didn't see why my staying home was such a

big deal. But I knew it wouldn't do any good to argue. Mom was so conscientious and so good at everything. She could never understand why other people weren't like her.

"Come on, girls, get dressed. I'll start loading the car. This is going to be one busy day."

I scrambled into my clothes and hurried out to the car where Mom and Trish were waiting impatiently. When we arrived at the park, Mr. Yokomura, Andy, and the other workers were bustling around getting breakfast started. Mr. Yokomura was also in charge of the big barbeque and chili dinner that night. You could never call him irresponsible. I hadn't realized how hungry I was until I smelled the ham and potatoes frying. Then I remembered that I hadn't eaten any dinner the night before.

The park tables and benches were still wet, and Andy was wiping them off. Before I could eat, I had to help him.

As I walked over to him, I avoided his eyes. "Good morning," I said.

Without any greeting at all, he growled. "Why didn't you come to the phone last night?"

"I was tired."

"The way you took off after dress rehearsal,

we were all worried about you."

"I—I just didn't want to face anybody after I ruined the play," I said.

"You didn't ruin it. That's why we have dress rehearsals—to fix anything that goes wrong."

"But the paper will give it a rotten review, and nobody will come, and it'll be my fault."

"Oh, for gosh sakes, Megan. You—"

"Andy? Come help me," Mr. Yokomura called. "Customers are here!"

We didn't have another chance to talk. All of a sudden the park was swarming with people. Festival Week was big. People came from all over the county. For the next week, the population of San Angelo would double.

Helen Mae was supposed to meet me at one o'clock so we could get ready for the parade. During the morning, she helped her mom at the candy booth. She came running up and waved a newspaper in my face.

"Read this!" she cried, and held out the amusement page.

"If it's the review, I don't think I want to see it," I said.

"Read it."

I sat on a bench and began to read. The first part told what the play was about. Then Chris was singled out as an excellent actor. The rest of the cast were lumped together.

"Now, read down here," Helen Mae said, pointing to a paragraph near the bottom of the article.

> A new comedy star is born. Megan Steele, who plays Mrs. Palmeteer, is hilarious as the kooky medium. Not once did she fall out of character, not even when the usual dress rehearsal disasters struck. She has a wonderfully expressive face. But what is most unusual in amateur theatre is to find someone with perfect comedy timing. I hope we'll be seeing more of this young talent.

Open-mouthed, disbelieving, I looked up at Helen Mae. "Is he talking about—me?"

"Is there another Megan Steele in town? Of course it's you. I was laughing so hard last night, I kept losing my place in the playbook."

"I thought I was awful," I said. I started to reread the part about me, but my mind drifted off . . . .

Megan Steele, the toast of Broadway, tries to leave the theater but sees the huge crowd waiting for her autograph. She slips out the back way. Waiting for her is a young man dressed in black. His face is hidden in the shadows. Instead of handing her something to autograph, he holds out a single, perfect red rose. He bows, then disappears into the night.

"Megan!" Helen Mae said. "How many times are you going to read it?"

I came back to the real world with a start. "May I keep the paper?" I asked. "I want to show it to Mom and Trish and Andy."

She nodded. "But I'll bet your mom buys every paper that was printed."

"I'll be right back," I said. "Then we can go get ready for the parade."

I tried to find Andy, but he'd gone back to the Palace for supplies. Mom was talking to the Mayor, and Trish was surrounded by the princesses and admirers.

I felt only a little let down. After that review, my feet weren't touching the ground.

* * * * *

At the parade, though, I came down to earth with a thud—or a plop!

Helen Mae and I, dressed as clowns, had to follow the horses, pick up their droppings with a shovel, and throw the droppings into a cart. I have to tell you, I was really, really glad there weren't any elephants in the parade.

My sister got to ride on a float with the

other princesses. Chris was riding in the lead car, because his mother was the one who got Terrence Whittaker, the movie star, to be the Grand Marshal. Of course, Carla got to ride in the second car because her dad was the mayor. Right behind Helen Mae and me, Spud was riding on a float sponsored by his parents' motel. Andy was making pizzas atop Mr. Yokomura's award-winning float. How he managed to throw the pizza dough into the air and catch it again on that bumpy parade route, I'll never know.

The cart Helen Mae and I had to use was pulled by a goat—a smelly, disagreeable, noisy goat. Every time I'd get a shovel full of droppings and start to toss them into the cart, that dumb goat would move just enough to make me miss. I swear, he did it on purpose. I must have picked up the same shovelful six times.

The crowd was rooting for the goat. We got more applause than even the movie star. Maybe they had all read the review and thought it was a comedy act.

Actually, I was kind of enjoying it. The laughter, the clip-clop of the horses' hooves, and the lilting music of the calliope in the band made me feel happy. Little kids with balloons and noisemakers yelled and laughed as we passed by. Some of them even came up to touch me like I was some kind of a celebrity.

I was really getting into the spirit of the festival when the band stopped in front of the viewing stand. The horses were just behind the band. When the drums, horns, and cymbals began to play, I think the horses got nervous. Helen Mae and I had to keep shoveling like mad.

The day was sunny, but there was still rainwater in some of the larger potholes. I threw a shovelful of droppings at the cart. The goat moved forward and spooked the horse in front of him. The horse wheeled around and knocked over the cart, which banged into me. I lost my balance, skidded on the droppings and ended up in the mud puddle.

The crowd roared.

Spud leaned over the side of the float behind us and yelled loud enough for everybody in the state to hear.

"Megan the Klutz strikes again!"

Nine

AFTER the parade, I changed into dry clothes. Then Helen Mae and I joined the other kids. By that time, everybody had read the review.

"I think it stinks," Carla said. "The reviewer should have said something about each one of us."

"Maybe he figured if he couldn't say something good, he wouldn't say anything," Spud told her.

Carla glared at him. "Well, getting stuck in the restroom made me so upset I couldn't think straight. And then Megan threw me off by doing all those stupid things and hiding the pen. Tonight will be different."

"It was funny," Andy said. "The audience thought it was all part of the play."

I wanted to talk about something besides the play. The giant bird was already beginning to flap around in my stomach again. "Do you think anybody ever gets over being nervous before a play?" I asked.

Spud laughed. "Just picture everybody in the audience in their underwear."

"I think it's good to be a little nervous just before a play starts," Chris said.

"You know, you sure look lousy," Spud said to Chris with his usual tact.

Chris did look awful. He hadn't touched his food. He was just slumped on the bench, leaning on his elbow. "Are you sick?" I asked.

"I haven't felt very well all day. Is it just me, or is it hot?"

Carla reached over and felt his forehead. "Chris, you're burning up. I hope you aren't getting the flu."

"I don't think so," Chris said. "I have a rash on my chest and back."

"Oh, no," Helen Mae said. She quickly got up and went over to Chris. "Let me see your chest."

Chris made a feeble attempt to be funny by holding his shirt closed and pretending to be embarrassed.

"Come on, Chris, let me look at you."

Chris lifted up his monogrammed white polo shirt.

"Oh, no," Helen Mae said again as she

inspected his chest and back. "I was afraid of that. You have chicken pox."

"Chicken pox!" Carla cried. "You kissed me last night! Chris, how could you do that to me?" She moved as far away from him as she could.

"I didn't feel all that bad last night," he said.

"Didn't you have chicken pox when you were a little kid?" Andy asked.

Chris shook his head. "I don't think I was ever exposed before. I wasn't around a lot of little kids."

I looked at Helen Mae. Her brother had come down with chicken pox yesterday. He and Chris had probably been exposed at the same time. So when were they together? I didn't bring it up then in front of the others, but I planned to find out what was going on.

"Chris, I think you ought to go home and go to bed," Andy said. "I'll find somebody to take you."

"But what about the play tonight?" Chris asked.

"Andy, you ought to be able to do Chris's part," I said. "You've been in lots of plays."

"I don't know the lines. I could read it from the playbook, but I'm the only one who can run the lights and—"

107

"I know the ghost's part," Spud said quietly.

"You're kidding," Carla said.

"I'm the prompter, remember?" Spud began to recite Carla's first speech. "I have a great memory. I know everybody's lines."

"If you think I'm going to kiss you," Carla said huffily, "you'd better think again."

"We don't have a whole lot of choices here," he said. "Maybe you'd rather play both parts yourself?"

"I suppose you're better than nothing," she said sarcastically.

Spud leered. "We really need to rehearse, especially the kiss."

Carla threw a piece of bread at him. I thought they deserved each other.

* * * * *

After Chris left, we all argued for a while about what to do next. We finally settled on the carnival. We bought cotton candy. I hate the stuff. But I ate some anyway, and it made me feel queasy. We threw darts and rings, shot at mechanical ducks, and tossed baseballs at the dunking booth. Andy and Helen Mae won adorable little stuffed animals at the dart-throwing booth. I won a really ugly ceramic dog at the archery concession.

I was having a great time, though. Spud wasn't obnoxious, and Carla wasn't sarcastic. The only thing spoiling the day was Chris not being with us.

"Let's go on some rides," Spud said. "After the pie-eating contest, I won't dare ride on anything."

We trooped over to the midway. Somehow, Andy and I ended up in the same seat on the giant ferris wheel.

"Aren't you afraid to ride with me?" I asked him. "We're liable to get stuck or something."

"I'll take the chance," he said.

When our seat reached the top, the wheel stopped for a minute. We swung gently in the breeze. An escaped balloon floated past. I looked down over the park and the river and at all the people having fun. The music of the merry-go-round and the squeals of children sounded far away.

I could feel Andy's eyes on me.

"You look different lately, Megan," he said finally.

"It must be my new haircut."

"No . . . it's more than that. Helen Mae seems different, too. I've been trying to figure it out."

I was kind of surprised that his mother hadn't told him she'd been coaching Helen

Mae and me. But I was glad she hadn't.

"You seem more—confident, more relaxed."

"You said that being in the play would help me."

"Sure, but I didn't expect it to happen so fast. We've only had one performance."

I grinned at him. "I'm a fast learner." Then more seriously, I said, "Your mom has helped Helen Mae and me a lot. She's given us a lot of tips on makeup and hair—things like that."

"I like your hair." Then he looked embarrassed and added quickly, "That ponytail you used to wear made you look like a skinned rabbit."

"Thanks a bunch," I said, pretending to be upset, but inside I was pleased. At least Andy had noticed the change in me.

"Megan, about the ball next Satur—"

"Hey, you guys," Spud called from the seat just below us. "Meet us at the river for a canoe ride."

"Okay," Andy yelled back.

"What about the ball?" I asked.

"Oh, nothing. Mom is chairperson for the dance committee," he said, but I had the feeling that he'd intended to say something quite different. I knew he wasn't going to ask to take me. No one in our group ever went to dances in couples unless they were going steady. Well, maybe he'd tell me later.

The giant wheel stopped, and we jumped off and headed for the river. We rode in a canoe. And would you believe it, it didn't tip over!

*   *   *   *   *

Later, we watched Spud win the pie- and cake-eating contest. Helen Mae and I entered the three-legged race and nearly ended up with three broken legs. The five of us were on the winning tug-of-war team, but poor Spud wasn't much help after eating so much.

By then we were getting really tired.

"I'm ready to go home and rest for a while before the play," Spud said, looking slightly pale.

"Me, too," Carla moaned. "I'm exhausted."

"I have to break the news about Chris to Mom," Andy said. "I'll see you guys tonight."

"Anybody want to come with me to the art display?" I asked. Mom had a sculpture in the arts and crafts competition. I wanted to see if she'd won a ribbon.

"Sure, I'll come," Helen Mae said.

We headed for the large tent. As soon as we were alone, I asked Helen Mae about her brother and Chris both getting chicken pox at practically the same time.

"I guess it happened when Chris and I went skating a couple of weeks ago."

"And your little brother went along?"

"Well . . . no. Chris came back to the house for a while. He played games with the little kids. You should have seen him. I guess he's never had much family."

A stab of jealously twisted my stomach. "So how come you didn't tell me?" I tried to keep my voice from showing I was hurt.

"I started to a dozen times, but you've been so involved in the play . . . ." Her voice trailed off.

"I think when a person has a best friend that the other person would tell them if another person—oh, you know what I mean."

Friendless and lonely, the young woman walks along the river's edge. Near a waterfall, a fine mist mingles with her tears.

"Megan don't be mad. It wasn't a date. All we talked about was the skating routine we were doing."

"It's okay," I said. "I was just upset because you didn't tell me."

"It's not me he likes, it's my family. I know it's hard to believe, but I honestly think Chris is lonely."

We'd been talking and almost walked past the large arts and crafts tent. Hardly anybody was looking at the displays. Mom hadn't let Trish or me see her entry, but I found it easily. It was a clay sculpture of Trish and me. I ran my fingers over the blue ribbon. She won first prize nearly every year.

Suddenly Helen Mae yelled from across the room, "Megan! Come quick!"

I thought she must have hurt herself. In my rush to get to her, I bumped against the table. Mom's sculpture wobbled. My heart did a double flip. I grabbed for the model and caught it just as it started to fall. Very carefully, I set it back in its place.

"What's wrong?" I asked as I hurried over to Helen Mae.

"Look at this. You've won a ribbon."

"Not me. I didn't enter anything."

"The card has your name on it."

"It has to be a mistake. I didn't—" I stopped as I saw my rocks. There was Guthrie the Camelpotamus along with Gertrude and the two babies. "How did they get here?"

"Megan, did you really paint them? They're adorable. How did you manage to make a rock look so cuddly?"

Mrs. Baxter, who was in charge of the exhibit, came up. "Megan, I'm glad to see you're following family tradition."

"Do you know who brought in these rocks?"

I asked, still puzzled.

"Of course, dear. Your sister, Patricia brought them in. She said you didn't have a chance to bring them yourself."

Trish? I wondered how long she'd known about the rocks.

"What a talented family," Mrs. Baxter said.

"But these are just silly little things I paint in my spare time."

"Oh, no, my dear. There is nothing silly about them. They are true art."

I must have been grinning like an idiot. The review about me had been terrific, but this blue ribbon meant a whole lot more.

Ten

OPENING night was even more hectic than the dress rehearsal, especially with Spud taking over for Chris.

When I was waiting for the curtain to go up, I peeked out to see if we had a full house. I was sorry I had. The sight of all those people turned my legs to fudge ripple.

Once I was on stage, though, I felt wonderful. It was a funny thing about acting. One part of my mind was saying the lines and really feeling like Mrs. Palmeteer. The other half was thinking about how the audience was laughing, whether Mom was enjoying the play, and why I hadn't eaten something. I was afraid my stomach might growl at the wrong time.

Spud was great. I couldn't believe he could come on at the last minute and be so good. Poor Carla, maybe because she was trying too hard, was awful. She overacted and sounded phony . . . except when she had to kiss Spud. I nearly broke up when Spud grabbed her and bent her backwards. He definitely took advantage of the situation. I mean, he really kissed her. And then he ad-libbed, "Sorry, Cecily, but we ghosts don't have too many opportunities, you know."

After the play, we had to take four curtain calls. Spud and I got the most applause. I loved it. It was even better than some of my daydreams.

Andy whispered to me, "You were a long way from the Letty Lettuce of the old days."

In the dressing room, Mrs. G gave us a little speech.

"I've put on a lot of plays in my day, but I can't remember being any prouder than I was tonight. I'm sorry Chris isn't here to share this moment. Every one of you, from prompters to prop people to the leads, worked long and hard. We're sold out every night of Festival Week."

We all clapped and hooted.

Megan Steele, the bright new star of Broadway, is playing to standing room only crowds . . . .

People came backstage to say how much they enjoyed the play. Mom and Trish each gave me a hug. "You were wonderful, honey," Mom said.

Trish whispered so that no one but me could hear. "I thought you were the best one in the play."

"It was the part," I said, trying to be modest, but I was practically bursting inside. "Anyone could play the medium."

And then it struck me. Not one single solitary thing had gone wrong. The klutz was dead—or at least she was on her way out.

* * * * *

The weather stayed great throughout Festival Week until the last day. It rained hard before the night of the ball.

I'd been looking forward to the dance with a mixture of excitement and nervousness.

Helen Mae came over to my place so we could get ready together. Trish came into my room to help us. She was already wearing her gown from the contest. She really looked beautiful, like the golden girl in my fantasy. Her gleaming blond hair, super tan, and beige lace gown made her eyes show up like sea-green jewels.

"That was really neat of you to enter Megan's rocks in the competition," Helen Mae said to Trish. "I just love Guthrie."

Trish and I had already talked about it. She'd said my rock animals were too good to keep hidden away. Now she put her arm around me. "I envy you, Megan."

She envied me?

"I'd give anything if I could paint like Dad," Trish said. She bit her lower lip, and in a husky voice asked, "Are you two going to the ball in those jeans?"

I gave her a quick hug. For a sister she wasn't so bad after all.

Helen Mae finished dressing first. "How do I look?" she asked, twirling around.

I'd been with her practically every day, but I hadn't realized how much weight she'd lost. "You look wonderful," I told her. "The dress is perfect." It was an off-the-shoulder, pale rose taffeta that made her skin look pink. "I'll bet Chris asks you to dance every dance."

Her face turned pinker than ever. "Not with Carla around, he won't."

"I'm glad Carla wasn't old enough to compete in the Miss San Angelo contest this year," Trish said ruefully. "I wouldn't be queen now." Then she looked at Helen Mae and me. "Come to think of it, I'm glad neither of you were in the competition."

Helen Mae and I looked at each other and

giggled like two silly little kids.

I slipped my dress over my head and got my hair caught on the hook. I groaned disgustedly. Nothing had changed.

Trish helped me get loose. I smoothed the dress over my hips and stood in front of the dresser mirror. The gown was pretty. We'd bought it at the same bridal shop where Trish had found hers. The sky blue made my eyes look blue instead of hazel. I thought I looked pretty good until Trish stood beside me and I compared our reflections in the mirror.

Mom poked her head into the room. "Are you girls about read—?" She stopped. "You all look wonderful. Let me get my camera."

"Oh, Mom there isn't time," I said. I hated to have my picture taken. I always looked like I belonged on the wall of the post office.

"You're right," Mom said. "I have to get to the gym and help take tickets."

Trish was going with her boyfriend, Larry. They were senior king and queen of the ball. The junior prince and princess would be chosen at the ball. Girls would vote for the prince, and the guys would vote for the princess.

As we were coming out to the car, I saw Spud standing in his driveway, but I almost didn't see the huge mud puddle in front of me.

"There she goes again!" Spud called.

I caught my balance, carefully sidestepped the puddle, and climbed into the car.

Score one for Megan—zip for the klutz.

* * * * *

The gym looked great, like a real ballroom with colored lights. A band from Los Angeles was playing a slow song. The place was crowded. I think every kid in town had shown up—even the guys. The girls love formal dances, but most of the guys hate them.

Andy's mom was taking the ballots at the door. I wrote Chris's name on the slip of paper and dropped it into the box. Helen Mae finished hers, then said, "Hey, look. There's Carla and Chris over by the refreshment stand. Let's join them."

"Sure," I said, "I'm thirsty." I really wasn't.

Carla had on a white and silver dress that made her look at least sixteen. Even with a few chicken pox scabs, Chris was definitely the best-looking guy in the room.

The master of ceremonies introduced Trish and Larry, then they danced alone with a spotlight on them.

The band played a few songs before the master of ceremonies announced that the

ballots had been tabulated for the junior
prince and princess.

I glanced over at Carla. She had a little
smile of anticipation on her face. Chris looked
uncomfortable.

There was a drum roll, then came the
announcement.

"This year's junior prince is none other
than—Christopher Rhodes! Come on up here,
Chris."

Chris looked at us, grinned, and hurried up
on stage.

"And this year's princess is—"

Carla set down her paper cup of punch and
looked poised to move.

"Megan Steele. Come on up here, Megan,
and join the prince."

For a moment I thought I was daydreaming,
then Helen Mae gave me a little push and
whispered, "Go on."

"But there must be a mistake," I said
weakly.

"Megan Steele, where are you? Your prince
is waiting."

In total shock, I walked up the steps to
stand beside Chris. I was sure there must have
been a mistake. Any minute they would
announce that Carla had really won.

The master of ceremonies placed a tiara on

my head, then Chris and I walked the million miles to the center of the gym for our spotlight dance. The band was playing another slow song.

The prince puts his arms around me, and we dance to the slow strains of the music. "You are so beautiful, Megan. I have worshiped you from afar . . . ."

When I felt Chris's arm around me, it was like my daydreams had become real.

"Dancing is pretty tame stuff after roller skating," Chris said. "You should see the new dance routine Helen Mae and I came up with."

This wasn't exactly the conversation of my dreams. And skating wasn't exactly my favorite subject.

"I can't believe I was chosen to be the princess," I said.

He went on talking about skating and Helen Mae. "The Vorcheks are a remarkable family, aren't they?"

"Remarkable," I said.

"And isn't that house of theirs great?"

"Yeah—great," I said. "Just great."

Before the spotlight dance was even over, Chris propelled me over to the refreshment table where Helen Mae and Carla were standing. Instead of being disappointed, I was almost relieved.

"Thanks for the dance, Megan," he said, then turned to Helen Mae. "How about the next one, Helena?"

They were barely out of hearing when Carla sputtered, "I can't imagine what he sees in Helen Mae. Oh, and by the way," Carla said sarcastically, "congratulations on being chosen the princess."

"I still can't believe it," I said.

"It's obvious that Andy stuffed the ballot box. After all, his mother was in charge of the voting."

I bristled. "You're nuts. Why would he do that?"

"Because he doesn't like me, that's why."

Anger boiled up inside me. How dare Andy do such a thing?

Just then Spud came up and asked Carla to dance.

"I wouldn't dance with you if you were the only boy here."

And they were off, arguing again.

"Spud, where's Andy?" I asked.

"I haven't seen him since you went up on stage. Come on, Carla, let's boogie."

I made my way through the crowd but couldn't see Andy anywhere. When I came back to where I'd started, Helen Mae and Chris were drinking punch.

"Have you guys seen Andy?" I asked.

They both shook their heads.

"Oh, Megan," Helen Mae said, "I'm really happy that you were voted the princess."

"That's what I want to talk to Andy about." I told them what Carla had said about Andy stuffing the ballot box.

"That's crazy," Helen Mae said. "He likes you a lot, but he'd never cheat."

"I agree," Chris said. "Andy's not like that."

"Andy's not like what?"

I whirled around to see Andy grinning at me. "Andrew Lloyd Gerritson, did you fix it so I'd win tonight?"

"No, you got it all on your own."

"I couldn't have. I'm not popular. I'll bet half the kids don't even know who I am."

"After the hit you made in the play everybody in town knows you."

"Yeah?"

"Yeah. Come on, let's dance."

I let him pull me out onto the dance floor. The band was playing another slow song. "Are you really telling the truth?" I asked.

"Well, I did think about stuffing the ballot box. I knew how you would have loved to be princess with Chris as your prince."

I looked back at Helen Mae and Chris. They were holding hands.

"I guess my dreams weren't very realistic," I said, nodding toward Chris and Helen Mae. "In my fantasies, not only do I get the handsome prince, but I'm also beautiful, talented, and definitely not a klutz."

"I don't think you are a klutz anymore," Andy said.

"Right. In fact," I said, teasing him, "I'm thinking of asking Mr. Yokomura for a job tossing pizzas into the air."

He stopped dancing and just stared at me for a second. "I don't think you're ready for that yet. I'M not ready for that!"

We started dancing again. Pretending it was an accident, I stepped on his toes—hard. "Oh, I'm so sorry, Andy. I guess once a klutz, always a klutz."

He grinned. "I suppose I'll just have to get used to it."

We danced for a little bit without talking. Then Andy said, "You look nice tonight, Megan."

For once, I really looked at him. "You, too," I said.

And he did. Maybe he wasn't a hunk like Chris, but he was fun to be with and easy to talk to. And I didn't have to try to impress him.

The beautiful princess in the blue gown looks

*up into the prince's gray eyes. As he bends
toward her, a lock of sandy hair falls over his
forehead. His lips touch hers . . .*

I drew back and looked up into Andy's gray
eyes. The dream and reality were the same.

About the Author

ALIDA YOUNG and her husband live in the high desert of Southern California. She gets many of her story ideas while hiking in the early morning. She says there is no one around to bother her except the desert animals. Once she came eyeball to eyeball with a large coyote. They looked at each other for a long moment, then he loped off into the brush. "He wasn't scared at all."

"I've always loved novels," she says. "I think I was about ten when I decided to read every book in our library. It took me three years just to get through the A's. It was then I decided if I ever wrote a book I'd change my name to Aaron Aardvark so my book would be the first one on the shelf."

Mrs. Young says, "I'm the original klutz. Once, I sprayed my husband's shirt with window cleaner instead of spray starch. Another time, instead of using hair spray, I spritzed my hair with deodorant. I used to perform in plays, and many of the things that happened to poor Megan, happened to me."

Other books by Alida Young include *I'll Be Seeing You, What's Wrong With Daddy?* and *Why Am I Too Young?*